HE STEPPED TOWARD me, closer, closer, stopping my thoughts dead. We stared at each other, and for once I didn't fill the silence with inane babbles.

"I don't think . . . ," I finally whispered.

"Good," he said. "Don't think."

"No," I whispered. "I mean . . ."

"Shhh. Can I kiss you?" he asked, his face so close to mine I could feel the heat from it on my cheeks. "I really want to kiss you."

I don't think so.

Not a good idea.

What if your sister sleepwalks?

I'm not even sure if I actually like you.

Kissing you outside that other time practically wrecked my life.

Who are you to me?

We shouldn't.

"Yes," I said.

novels by
RACHEL VAIL:

The Avery sisters trilogy

LUCKY

GORGEOUS

BRILLIANT

NEVER MIND!

IF WE KISS

YOU, MAYBE:
The Profound Asymmetry of Love in High School

JUSTIN CASE:
SCHOOL, DROOL, AND OTHER DAILY DISASTERS

JUSTIN CASE:
SHELLS, SMELLS, AND THE HORRIBLE FLIP-FLOPS OF DOOM

kiss me again

RACHEL VAIL

An Imprint of HarperCollinsPublishers

To Mitch, again and always

HarperTeen is an imprint of HarperCollins Publishers.

www.epicreads.com

Library of Congress Cataloging-in-Publication Data
Vail, Rachel.
    Kiss me again / Rachel Vail. — 1st ed.
        p.   cm.
    Summary: Having once shared a kiss with her best
friend's boyfriend, Kevin, fourteen-year-old Charlie finds life
even more awkward when their parents marry, making Kevin,
still her crush, now her stepbrother.
    ISBN 978-0-06-194719-3
    [1.   Stepfamilies—Fiction.   2.   Dating   (Social
customs)—Fiction.   3.   Interpersonal   relations—Fiction.
4.   Remarriage—Fiction.   5.   High   schools—Fiction.
6. Schools—Fiction.]   I. Title.
PZ7.V1916Kis   2013   2012011521
[Fic]—dc23   CIP
                                                          AC

Typography by Amy Ryan
13 14 15 16 17   LP/RRDH   10 9 8 7 6 5 4 3 2 1
❖
First paperback edition, 2014

kiss me again

one

I TRIED NOT to look at Kevin Lazarus's lips, or remember how they tasted.

He was not only my former crush but now also my stepbrother, among other complications. I had just deftly dodged the kiss he'd aimed at my mouth by jolting my face up a few inches and kissing his forehead.

Yeah. Practically a ninja, that's me. Quite the avoidance maneuver I'd pulled off there.

Wait. I kissed his forehead? Maybe that was a weird thing to do. Subtly but deeply weird. Like wearing a polo shirt buttoned all the way up.

A hint of a smile tipped up a corner of his mouth.

It occurred to me that I must have accidentally been looking a little bit at his lips, to notice that. Also that maybe I had accidentally said the thing about the polo shirt out loud, or that maybe he could read my mind. Or, maybe, he just wanted to smile because he was looking at me.

That thought made my fingers all go numb. They hung like swelling sausages from my hands. I sent up a silent prayer that he would not notice them and back away into the hallway, horrified, shrieking, "Ack! Sausage fingers!"

I decided to say a quick, firm *good night*. Kevin would get the hint and leave without seeing my fingers, and also without any other weirdness passing between us.

My mouth clearly did not get the memo. Instead of saying *good night*, it mirrored the semismile on Kevin's mouth.

"So . . . ," he breathed.

"Mmm," I answered, meaning mmm-hmm, as in *Yes*, like, *Wow, this is awkward*. But the *hmm* of the *mmm-hmm* got cut off, which made it more like a hum, more like *Mmm, yes, this is good*.

As I was panicking/overthinking this, a door closed down the hall. "What the . . ."

"Their door," Kevin whispered.

"Ew," I said, and then articulately added, "Ew, ew, ew." My mom and his dad, behind a closed door on their wedding night.

"Shhh." Kevin reached toward my head and touched a piece of hair that had sprung out of a twist from my wedding updo. He twirled it around his finger. This was a problem because I am apparently allergic to Kevin Lazarus twirling my hair. It makes breathing very difficult for me.

"I kissed George today," I announced.

"Okay," Kevin said. His cheeks blazed pink down near his jawline. He stopped twirling but kept hold of that strand of my hair. I made sure my head stayed steady so it wouldn't get yanked out of his fingers, though a part of me was like, *Okay? That's it? Okay?* Because he'd been ready to kiss me on the lips and maybe even tell me he loved me ten seconds earlier. But now he hears I had recently kissed another guy, and all he can say is *Okay?* Really?

See, I told myself. *This is why I like George so much better.* And our kiss, mine and George's, was actually perfect. Dappled sunlight, under a tree, music playing in the background. No twirled hair. No foreheads. No sausage fingers.

"At the wedding," I added, leaving off the dappled sunlight and other details. Overkill, I decided.

"I figured."

"We're not going out or anything," I said, cringing even as the hedging words left my mouth. "Officially. Me and, you know, George."

"No?"

"But I really like him. George." I considered waggling my sausage fingers at Kevin's blushing face, to drive him away from me. Like a hex. For everybody's protection. "A lot. I really like George."

"Mmm-hmm," Kevin answered. Which I have to say completely pissed me off.

"So," I said, willing myself not to add *And he really likes me—do you?* Or possibly, more honorably, *So get your darn non-sausagey fingers out of my hair.* "So we can't, you and I can't . . ."

"Can't what?" he asked, despite the fact that we were standing so close we could smell the Crest on each other's breath.

"This," I whisper-yelled back. "This, whatever. Don't act like . . . This. Together." If I sneezed, he'd get knocked out from the head clonk. *Can't what?* Please. Though, to be fair, I could have just walked away myself. If I fully meant it, about *we can't.* But I didn't want to be rude.

Or maybe we were magnets, me and Kevin, drawn irresistibly toward each other. Or maybe I was romanticizing and we were just two random ninth graders, overtired and confused and curiously addicted to flirting with each other.

"Okay," he said, but didn't step back, either. He might even have tipped a millimeter closer. If we simultaneously said the word *prune,* we'd be kissing.

Don't say prune, I warned myself.

"Okay?" I repeated instead. "Just—okay? You keep saying okay!" His hand fell to his side. My hair sagged in front of my eye. "You have to stop saying okay. Okay?"

"Okay." Microsmile. Damn.

"Seriously! I mean, do you, like, even want to kiss me? Or were you just . . ."

"Do you want to kiss me?" he whispered back. "You just said you and George . . ."

"That's right! Me and George. Yeah. And he, he, he really cares about me. He doesn't just twirl my hair around his little finger and make me go all wobbly. He makes me feel . . . sturdy, in fact."

"Sturdy?"

"Yeah," I said. "Sturdy."

"Sturdy is good."

"Yes, exactly—it is! He also . . . he listens."

"I'm listening."

"Not really. George is like—I made a random comment once about the weather report. George remembered, and he followed up on it."

"The weather report?"

"In a romantic way. Forget it."

"He was romantic about the weather report?"

"Never mind. What I mean is, unlike you, George doesn't—"

"Doesn't make you feel wobbly."

I blinked. My eye juice had all dried up. I force-blinked a few more times, even though the insides of my eyelids had become sandpaper, so each blink scraped permanently disabling scratches into my corneas.

"That's not what I meant at all," I whispered.

"Charlie." He caught my chin with his upturned right palm.

My eyes closed.

I didn't think, *No, no, no, I cannot kiss this boy.*

5

I didn't think, *Wow, I really like kissing Kevin Lazarus.*

I didn't, for once, think anything.

I just felt my lips melting into the heat of Kevin's lips.

My eyes, opening slowly, met his.

His thumb swiped lightly down my cheek. "You make me feel wobbly, too," he whispered.

He walked slowly, silently down the hall. When he got to his door, he turned his face partway back to me. The smile on his mouth bloomed slowly. I watched it spread across the lips I'd just unforgivably been kissing. "See you in the morning," he whispered.

two

I WOKE UP tangled in my sheets, with morning light slanting through my window, and congratulated myself on the wisdom of waking up early to get ready. I checked my alarm clock.

10:23.

What? It didn't make any sense. I picked it up and shook it. Obligingly, it changed to 10:24.

"You are not helping," I muttered to it.

The post-wedding brunch was called for 10:30. I had a big six minutes.

I slipped into the bathroom, new clothes in hand, and locked the door behind me. Until the Lazarus family moved in, I had never even noticed if the bathroom door had a lock, never mind locked it. I took a really quick shower with a towel on my hair. There was new shampoo in there. Head and Shoulders. Well, okay, so. Kevin has dandruff, apparently. Too much information. His shampoo in my shower. Ugh, too weird.

I had to dry off all the way. No more air-drying for me. First time I'd ever gotten dressed in the bathroom, and seriously? It was humid.

I smudged a clear patch onto the fogged mirror to make sure I looked okay. A little discombobulated, but not awful, I decided.

Not as bad as the night I got home from Darlene Greenfudder's horrible house party back in early February, when I drunkenly blurted to Tess in front of everybody we were friends with that I had kissed her boyfriend, *Kevin Lazarus*, while our families were away in Vermont together over Christmas break.

I never want to look or feel like that again. I obviously should have just told Tess immediately after I first kissed Kevin outside school in October. She was my best friend; we were supposed to tell each other everything.

Tess said that night of the horrible party that our friendship was basically over, forever. She still wasn't hanging out with me or talking to me, but she had come by the wedding reception, on her bike. Though she said no to coming in and having something to eat, she did tell me to wish my mom good luck from her.

I took a deep breath and reminded myself that that was

something. And also that I had been in the bathroom for a very long time and my hair was starting to frizz. I smoothed my tight gray brunch dress down in front and took a breath before I flung open the door. I could hear people downstairs and out back already.

Not good. I never oversleep. I like to have time to myself before I face people.

As I got to the landing midstairs, Kevin's aggressively skinny grandmother smiled largely up at me and asked, "Do you know where they keep the bathroom?"

"Um," I said, thinking, *keep* it? Like a horse? Or a mistress?

"I know," she whispered conspiratorially. "Can you believe this house?"

I said, "Yeah." She had obviously forgotten who I was, despite all the mergers-and-acquisitions photos with both families the day before. "What a house."

She smiled even bigger, but just with her mouth. Her forehead and eyes didn't move one millimeter. "Well, I'll check upstairs. Are you a friend of Kevin's?"

"Um," I said, since I wasn't sure I had a good answer to that one, either.

"Charlie!" Mom yelled from the kitchen.

"That woman keeps screaming," the skinny grandma whispered on her way up my stairs. "Poor Joe. Well, his own fault. Made his bed."

"Didn't we all," I answered, hoping I had in fact remembered to make my bed, or at least close my door.

"Charlie!" Mom screamed.

When I got to the kitchen, Mom was standing at the counter, dental smiling—like the pictures after your braces come off, where you show all your teeth but no humor.

"Hi," I offered. "Nice party."

"Who are all these people?" she muttered.

I looked out at the deck, which was packed, and then toward the driveway, which was full of cars, mostly SUVs.

"Your friends?"

"Ha," she said. "My friends have never been on time to anything, never mind early. 'A few people,' he said."

Kevin's father had come up behind my mother. He mimed *Shhh* to me, and bent down to kiss my mother's neck, melting the tension there into taffy.

"Who are all these people?" he whispered, and she laughed, a more rumbling, low, and, honestly—as gross as this is—*sexy* new laugh, in response. My armpits burst into a sweat attack.

"We're out of coffee already," my mother whispered up at her new husband. It sounded like some sort of inside joke, some coded thing all cool and private between them, rather than like a grocery issue.

"Hey, Joe!" a guy called. He looked like a bald, muscle-bound version of Joe, leaning in from the deck with Joe's expression mirrored on his face. "Is there more coffee? We're empty back here. . . ."

"Working on it, Bill," Joe said.

"Uncle Bill?" I confirmed with Samantha, who was

10

leaning against the counter, watching me with her intense, unblinking eyes.

"My father's brother," Samantha whispered. She was chewing her cuticles. "He's a caffeine addict." Her eyes widened, as if she were saying he was a heroin addict.

"Ah," I said. "Watch out for Uncle Bill. Any of your friends here?"

Samantha shook her head, her pale face serious. "Besides my Betta fish, I only really have one, and he moved to Japan last year."

"Oh, that sucks," I said.

"Yeah," she whispered. "It does." A hint of a smile twitched her mouth. She was wearing a long black skirt and a lacy-collared shirt, with a zip-up greenish hoodie sweatshirt over it, and tube socks with black suede Merrells. I smiled back at her.

Meanwhile, my mother's head was tipped back onto Joe's shoulder, and they were smiling full out at each other, like isn't this the most romantic and private secluded beach honeymoon ever?

Joe said, "Kevin," without moving his eyes from my mother's. I half expected her to say, *Huh? What? My name is Elizabeth, not Kevin! There has been a horrible mistake—let us annul immediately!* But my witty mom had morphed into a romance caricature, so she just smiled dreamily. I suppressed a retch.

Kevin had a croissant, nabbed from the still-Saran-Wrapped tray, halfway into his mouth as his eyes flicked up to his father at the mention of his name. "Hmgh?" he responded, and a flurry of croissant snow-crumbs confettied out in front of his face like a blizzard.

Samantha and I both started laughing at that, which made Kevin choke a bit. That just got us laughing more.

"Kevin," Joe tried again. "Can you go get more coffee? Here's forty bucks—get two of those box things from Cuppa, okay? And bring me change. Take my bike."

"I hate your bike," Kevin said, grabbing the cash and shoving it into his pocket.

"It has a basket."

"That's why I hate it," he said.

Mom gave me a look. "Charlie can go with you," she offered.

"Mom!"

"Come on, Charlie," Kevin said. "Keep the change, you said, right?"

"Ahhh, no!" his father called after him, but he was laughing, so I couldn't be sure if he meant it or not.

I grabbed my bag off the hook and followed Kevin down the stairs through the basement, grumbling, "How did I get roped into this?"

"Please tell me you wouldn't rather stay here with all my relatives," he said, opening the door to the garage.

I hesitated.

"What?" he demanded.

"I'm thinking about it."

He gave me a wicked grin and turned away. "Where's your bike?"

"In the shop," I lied, because I didn't feel like going around back to jiggle it out of the shed. "Also, I'm wearing a dress."

"I noticed."

When normal people blush, their cheeks pink up a bit. My whole head lit up like a red version of Violet Beauregarde's, midmetamorphosis into a blueberry. I could feel it heating up the garage. *He noticed. He noticed my dress. He noticed I'm wearing it.*

I tried to talk my head into chilling by explaining to it that he had only meant that he noticed I was wearing a dress, no big deal—he hadn't, for instance, added that I looked hot in it or anything. There was truly no need for my head to go all aflame over such a thing. The fact that I was wearing a dress was not that huge a mystery to have uncovered.

"Do you want to take Samantha's bike?" he asked. "It might be a little small for you. . . ."

"Whatever," I said, trying to not look too hulkingly large, in case that was his point there.

"Take mine," he said. "I'll ride my dad's basket-case bike." He grabbed his father's blue, basket-bearing bike and headed toward the open garage door.

We stood side by side, clicking the buckles of our helmets under our chins.

"Ready?" he asked. He had already put one foot on a pedal and was zooming down the driveway with his other leg up in the air and then somehow over the seat, onto the other pedal, before he got to the bottom of the hill. "Come on, Charlie!" he called back to me.

My cell phone buzzed inside my bag. It was George, texting that he was sorry, he'd be a little late to the party but would be there as soon as he could. I texted him back not to rush, because I was heading out to Cuppa to buy more coffee for the caffeine fiends. I didn't mention that I was riding bikes there with Kevin, who was waiting for me down by the big evergreen at the bottom of the driveway.

I shoved my phone back into my bag without waiting for a response and slung the strap over my head, across my body. Then I gripped the handlebars and rode down the hill, toward the empty, quiet street and Kevin and everything else that was ahead.

three

KEVIN CHAINED THE two bikes to the bike rack together outside of Cuppa.

"Hey," he said when I started on shaking legs toward the door. I turned around to see what was up.

As a response, he touched my elbow.

"Kevin," I answered, my eyes darting around. "What are you—"

"Chuck," he whispered.

We were in public. Anybody could see us.

He smiled at me. "That was fun, last night."

"Yeah, well, now it's today."

"I know," he whispered. His fingers had dropped from my elbow, but he took a step closer to me. "But after we kissed, last night, I—"

"We shouldn't have. We can't. Ever." I turned away and walked toward Cuppa.

"Because of George?"

"Yeah. And also, everything . . ."

His right shoulder shrugged microscopically as he looked past me to the window of Cuppa. "They need help."

"What?" I turned and saw the HELP WANTED sign. "Oh. Well, don't we all."

"All what?"

"Want help," I said.

He smiled at that. My heart cramped up. Damn.

"Maybe I should try for the job."

"Don't you have to be older?" he asked.

I yanked the door open, wondering what it would be like to be older, cooler, working at Cuppa, knowing by then how to manage all my tumbling, tumultuous, unruly emotions.

The lady behind the counter was beautiful, like someone who had just come to life out of a painting—all cascading, reddish curls and pale skin, green eyes twinkling as she watched us approach.

"We need two boxes of coffee," Kevin said.

"Pretty thirsty," the lady guessed. "For here?"

"No, to go," Kevin explained.

"Okay," she said, and smiled. There was a small silver ring through her tongue. "You sure?"

"Oh," Kevin said. "Right. You knew that."

"I've been in the business awhile."

"You're just like Charlie," he said to the lady. "Two beats ahead of me at all times."

"We girls can't always slow down to boy speed. Hurts our engines." She winked at me. "Right, Charlie?"

"I thought we were gonna drink it here," I said.

Kevin's fingers touched my back, between my shoulder blades. A shiver radiated up and down my body from that point, like ripples on a pond from a dropped pebble—or glass hit by a thrown stone.

The tongue-pierced lady watched us while that was going on, while I tried to hide the shiver and keep my face blank and unreadable. I'm not sure I succeeded, because she tilted her head slightly at me, the way cats do when yarn jiggles near their faces, then turned her back to us, to fill up two big boxes with coffee.

I forced myself to take a deep breath and step forward, away from Kevin's lingering fingers. *Stop thinking about him! Focus. Where the hell even was I?*

I hadn't been inside Cuppa for almost three years, since Tess and I discovered it is apparently not a place for middle schoolers or even ninth graders unless you were extraordinarily cool. We were taught that fact by Tess's older sister, Lena, who had been interrupted from making out with her boyfriend in one of the two back booths. By us. She explained the rules of Cuppa while she escorted us out the door sideways, by our ponytails.

Tess and I could hardly stand up after Lena stormed back in, we were laughing so hard. We ended up holding on to each other with tears bubbling up in our eyes out there on the sidewalk.

"She *evicted us*!" Tess said.

"Like a couple of hoodlums!" I added, which just doubled us over more.

"Hoodlums!" Tess kept repeating. "HOODLUMS!"

It's a miracle we didn't pee in our pants right there. I wasn't sure if she was mocking me or not, but it didn't really matter; we were too in love with ourselves to care if people were staring at us. Let them stare. We were twelve and happy and best friends.

But there I was, nearly fifteen years old, and not with Tess but with Kevin. The ache of lack-of-Tess kicked my stomach. I leaned forward onto the counter.

"You okay?" Kevin whispered. "Need some water before we go home?"

"Home?" I repeated.

"What?"

"That might be the weirdest thing you ever said to me," I answered. "Home."

"So far," he said. "Give me time." He was smiling at me, calm and intense, deep into my eyes.

"Okay," I whispered.

Meanwhile, the Cuppa lady put the two boxes of coffee on the counter, along with a cup of water. I downed it while she took the money from Kevin, rang up the sale, and gave him change.

"I was wondering about the job," I told her.

"You were?"

"Yes," I said. "About, if I could please apply for it."

"How old are you?"

"Fifteen," I exaggerated, and then, when she and Kevin both looked skeptical, added, "Approximately."

"Uh-huh," the lady said. She handed me a pad and a pen.

I guess my look was blank.

"Give me your name and number. I'll call you for an interview."

"Okay." I wrote down my information and handed the pad and pen back. "Thanks," I said.

As I followed Kevin toward the door, holding one of the boxes, the woman said, "Charlie?"

I turned around.

"*Why* do you want the job?"

I stood there trying to think fast. *Spending money? Sure, though I don't have anything I'm desperate to buy.*

Because if I'm behind the counter at Cuppa, I won't have to feel abandoned when I come in here and see the table Tess and I picked out as our own and us not sitting at it? Well, yeah, that too.

I need a job here because . . . because I need to find someplace I can hide, since all my safe places are gone.

"A lot of reasons," I said instead. "I . . . well, I'm a,

interested in . . . want to . . ."

"Think about it," the Cuppa lady said. "My name is Anya. I'll call you."

"Oh, okay," I said. "Thanks, um, Anya." I had already blown my chance, obviously. I opened the door and Kevin stepped through it.

"A lot of reasons?" Kevin asked, unlocking our bikes.

"Shut up," I said. Which made him smile. Which I only let myself smile back at for two seconds. Three, tops.

four

WHEN WE GOT back with the coffee, some of my mom's friends had shown up, and a few of our relatives, to add to the hordes of Lazarus people and some kids from school. I went up to my room and changed out of my sweaty-armpit dress into jeans and a T-shirt, then ventured down to my basement, or what used to be *my* basement. Now, with the Lazarus pool table there and a lot of the boy population of ninth grade, it hardly felt like mine at all.

"Hey! Charlie!" It was Darlene Greenfudder, beaming at me.

"Hey!" I said back. "How's it going, Darlene?"

"Great," she said brightly. "Well, except my grandfather died."

"Oh my gosh," I said, stopping in the middle of the stairway. "I'm so sorry."

"Yeah, it was weird."

"Weird?"

"Totally. Right before he died, my grandfather, PawPaw, called me to his bedside and said, 'If the transmission is shot, doesn't matter how pretty the detailing is. That car is not running.'"

I was not at all sure how to respond to this. But Darlene was staring at me, impatient and expectant, her brown eyes heavily lined in sparkly purple pencil. So I said, "Wow. That's really . . . profound."

"Yeah, I know," she said, nodding. "And then he just, boom, died."

"Oooo," I said, praying that I would not start laughing. "Just, boom?"

Darlene nodded. "Boom."

I took a steadying breath and said, "Well, I'm so sorry."

A big giggle from the girls downstairs bubbled up. Darlene and I both smiled at them, by habit. Kevin caught my eye. His head tilted like a question, but what did he want, for me to go fawn all over him, too? How many of those girls were touching his arms, four? Five? Not that I was jealous. It had nothing to do with me. Obviously. I was actually scanning the room for George. And possibly Tess.

I turned back to Darlene instead, who was now waving at one of the smoker girls flopped with two others on my old beanbag chairs.

"Lots more people came than last time you had a party," Darlene pointed out.

I had to laugh a bit. You can't even get mad at somebody who just puts it right out there like she does.

"Because of Kevin." Darlene placed her hand consolingly on my shoulder. "You know how he is."

"Yeah," I said. "Sort of."

"Oh well," Darlene said cheerfully. "He was pretty demented by then."

"Kevin?"

"PawPaw. You know, the detailing? So, probably he was just nuts, but it sounded deep, and you're smart. I thought maybe you'd get it."

"Sorry," I said again.

"That's okay. It was worth a try. He didn't leave me anything in his will, because he was kind of a failure at everything he tried. But I thought maybe this was like a nugget of wisdom. Oh well. Like on *Antiques Roadshow*. Most of the time the stuff people bring in is crap, but once in a while there's some diamond in the buff."

"Rough," I corrected.

"What?"

"Diamond in the rough, I think." *Jeez Louise, can I please be normal for one full frigging minute?*

"Diamond in the *rough*? What does *that* mean?"

"No idea," I admitted, and forced myself to smile up at Darlene. "Maybe he thought you should get the oil checked or something. In your car. When you get one."

"Oh. Yeah, that's probably it."

She looked a little deflated, so I added, "That's really good advice, actually. To check the oil. I think. Hey, so, speaking of . . . non sequiturs, is Tess coming today?"

"No, she's still mad at you." She smiled sweetly at me. "Anyway. Thanks, Charlie. That's nice. Get the oil checked. Okay." She took a step down toward the basement, away from me.

"Cool," I said. "Thanks for coming today."

"Oh," said Darlene. "I figured this might be awkward, but . . ."

"Because of . . ." I tilted my head toward where Kevin stood, down in the basement. I had forgotten that she and Kevin had made out, even before I had kissed him. And he had broken up with her the next day online. He was not the nicest of guys, Kevin, which is why I had never liked him as a friend.

"Yeah," Darlene said. "That kind of sucked, what you did to Tess."

"Oh," I said. "That."

She nodded sympathetically. "I decided that it would be fine for me to come over when Kevin has a party. Pretty much everybody was coming, so it wouldn't make sense for me to boycott this, right?"

"Uhhh, I guess not."

"Right. You understand. It's not like I came here to hang out with you. So I'm not being, like, disloyal to Tess. Not really."

"Yeah," I said. "Don't worry about it."

"Thanks, Charlie. You're really nice. And, listen. Everybody's totally over it, other than Tess, of course. It's not like you're a piranha or anything."

"A piranha?"

"I'm improving my vocabulary. My mom's making me take a class, since I practically failed English last semester. *Piranha* means outcast."

I did not say, *No, you dolt, a piranha is not an outcast; a piranha is a fish with teeth. You mean a pariah.* I just said, "Oh." Which, I think, should give me some cosmic points. For not being a jerk. For gritting my teeth so hard to resist uttering a necessary but jerkish vocabulary correction that I may actually have ground down my molars a bit.

"I better go in. . . ."

"Sure. Sorry about your grandfather," I said again, keeping my sharp piranha teeth to myself.

"Oh! Thanks," Darlene said, smiling in a truly friendly way. "Sorry about your, you know . . ."

"Life," I finished for her, and slumped down to sit on the stairs. *So this is how it's going to be,* I thought. *I am basically a piranha.*

It did not help to know that Tess would have pretty much laughed her head off about Darlene's earnest confusion, and then probably would have bought me a pet piranha, to celebrate my new mascot. Or at least a T-shirt with a piranha on it.

It was one of those moments when missing Tess took all

my energy. I had to just slump amoeba-ishly on the stairs until the spasm passed.

The party ground on and on. I took a short break in my room but then forced myself out again. I did not want to be that much of a cliché, in my room with the door closed during a party. I mean, seriously. I am a ninth-grade girl, I admit it, but I have some pride, at least about not being completely frigging *obviously* a ninth-grade girl. I went back downstairs with my piranha grin showing.

People were still there, milling around. My friend Jennifer was there, over in the corner, chatting with Kevin's best friend, Brad. Jennifer's parents are close with Kevin's dad, so of course, her whole family was at the party, but still I was happy to see a friendly face. No Drama Jen. She used to hang with me and Tess when me and Tess were me-and-Tess, and she has stayed good friends with both of us. I made a vow to be more like Jennifer, except athletically (lack of talent on my part would make that pretty impossible), as I smiled at her. She smiled back and lifted her hand in a friendly hey-there type of wave. *Ah, Jen. You are my new role model. Gonna be like you, less lurchy and jerky and stressed.* I picked some pretzels off the pool table surface and headed toward her.

As I made my way to the corner where she stood, Kevin slid by me and whispered into my neck, "You changed."

"Just my personality," I whispered back.

He didn't laugh. "Your dress," he clarified, turning away, swept up immediately into a group with Brad and other boys from the soccer team. All around us, ninth graders, some of whom I'd known since kindergarten, chatted in small groups, laughed together, smiled with braced or newly unbraced teeth at one another. I stood there alone for a moment, a rock in the rapids.

And there was George. Ahh, finally. George, the nicest guy ever, the guy I'd kissed less than twenty-four hours earlier, making his way across the basement toward me.

"Hey," he said.

"Hi there," I said.

"How you holding up?"

"My head's kind of spinning," I whispered.

"I bet," George said, and put his heavy arm around me. I leaned against him, took a few deep breaths, and didn't look over to see if Kevin was noticing. I breathed in the clean laundry smell of George, rested on the solidity of him. He wasn't grabbing at my hair, wasn't searching my eyes with pain and vulnerability twinkling in his. He just stood there, warm and clean and patient. I closed my eyes. My pulse wasn't racing, it was slowing. Ahhh. I could fall asleep standing there and he'd just let me doze. If the party ended and I was snoozing against him, George would stay standing there, his empty plastic cup in his hand, holding me up.

I slung my arm around his waist, opened my eyes, and smiled up at him. "Longest twenty-four hours ever," I whispered.

"Sure," he whispered back. "You okay?"

Damn. Why does that question make me start to spurt tears?

"You want to get some air, talk or something?"

"No," I said. "I'm good. Everything is good." As I flashed my piranha smile up at George, I saw Kevin turn his face toward Brad, away from me. Had he been watching me? I grabbed hold of George's hand and squeezed. "Listen, George, I'm really glad we . . ."

He squeezed back. "Me too."

So that was that, and nothing more had to be said between us. We talked to pretty much everybody, and held hands almost the entire time. When the party was petering out, I walked him to the back door. He handed me a small box. "Sorry I was late today," he said. "I had to wait for the store to open to get you this."

"What is it?" I asked, opening it. Inside was a pair of earbuds. "Um, wow. Okay. Thanks, George."

"I figured you're used to privacy, and now, with the Lazarus family all in your space, you might need to . . . sometimes . . . retreat."

I clutched the earbuds, pink with red polka dots, to my chest. "Yes," I said, and hugged George without caring who saw, or if anybody did.

five

THE AWKWARDNESS OF breakfast the next day, when it was finally just the five of us left in the house, was bad enough. The fact that my mother and her new husband were glowing—seriously, emitting light you could read by, if their sheepish grins weren't so frigging distracting—was pretty near unbearable.

Being the last one down to breakfast only added to my disorientation. I stood at the door of the kitchen, staring at all these people, a major crowd for me to confront on a Monday morning in my unshowered, unfed state. So many people in my kitchen. *The parties are over! When is everybody going to leave already?*

Oh, right. Never.

For the rest of my life, we were always going to have company.

It took me a minute to figure out what the conversation was. It sounded like Joe and Samantha were talking in some kind of code made of numbers. Kevin had his bio textbook out and open in front of him.

"Kevin's next, then you, Charlie," Joe practically sang at me.

"To . . . what?"

"Go over your work," he said, like that was the most obvious thing. "Get ready for the day."

I almost turned toward Kevin to roll my eyes at him, to check if this was standard operating procedure in his family, because it sure as hell was NOT in mine, but then, at the last second, decided that actually I was not prepared to bond with Kevin at all or especially in front of anybody, thanks.

In fact, at that moment I made what seemed to me to be a completely brilliant if obvious plan: not to look at Kevin at all. Ever again in my entire life.

It would just make things cleaner.

"No, thanks, I'm all set," I said in what sounded to me at least like a pretty steady, respectful but definite voice, and then sat down at the table in front of my bowl full of not-cereal.

"Good way to start the day," Joe insisted, holding a half gallon of orange juice in each hand. "Get your brain in gear. Pulp or no pulp?"

"Pulp, please. What *is* this?" I asked, staring down at the lumpy mess in my bowl, where raspberries, nuts, and some stray, escaped cereal were in their death throes, drowning in yogurt.

"Special treat," my mother's newly minted husband happily announced while pouring juice into my glass, and then added, "It's a parfait."

"Well," I said, unable to hold in my horribleness any longer. "Isn't that just *très parfait*?"

Joe laughed. Then he stood up and went to my mother, who was silently struggling over the complications of making coffee in their new wedding-gift coffee/cappuccino maker. Mom turned to look out the kitchen window instead of at my pleading face, holding her empty *Number 1 Mom* mug that I had gotten her for Mother's Day a hundred years ago. Kevin turned a page of his bio textbook, I saw with my distractingly good peripheral vision. When the coffee machine started burbling all proudly, Joe leaned against the counter beside Mom and continued talking in number code with Samantha. Times tables, I belatedly recognized. Cute.

My cell phone buzzed in the pocket of my fleece.

Tess, I thought. *Perfect timing and thank goodness, because I really need to talk to you.* She had sworn she'd never forgive me, even defriended me on Facebook, but I still maintained a tiny sliver of hope, and here she was. . . .

I slipped my buzzing phone out of my pocket as casually as possible, because my mother doesn't like phones at the table.

The text was from Kevin, who was hunched over his parfait, studying the bio homework, or seeming to.

The text said:

Ain't breakfast swell?

I managed to not laugh. At least, not out loud.

"I gotta go," I said, shoving my cell in my pocket and my chair away from the table.

"You have to eat breakfast," Joe said.

I stopped but didn't turn back to him. "No," I said. "I don't."

On my way up the stairs, I typed fast with my thumbs:

Pretty slick texting there, bucko.

"You'll be hungry," Mom called after me, as if she had ever monitored my breakfast intake in the past three years.

"I'll be fine!" I yelled back.

I ran up to my room, grabbed clothes, dumped them on the bathroom floor, and locked the door before I allowed myself to check and see if he had texted back yet. Yes:

Rbay.

Sorry, rbay? Uh, sorry, Kevin, never got that vocab word. Rbay?

I showered aggressively, shaving so fast I nicked each leg and had little rivulets of blood tracing streams down my legs after I shut off the water.

It was only as I combed through the tangles in my hair that I figured out *rbay* had to mean *right back at you.*

Is that like a common acronym, or did he make that up on the spot? Just for me? Or does everybody use *rbay*? I yanked my clothes onto my still slightly damp body. Urgh. No time for much else, so I pulled my hair back into a ponytail and grabbed my bag with my books that nobody was quizzing me on, thanks, and scuffed down the steps.

Joe was supervising Samantha's dishwashing while Mom sat at the table reading the paper. Kevin was at the door. My cell phone, in my pocket, buzzed again.

"Ready?" Kevin asked me out loud.

"Not even close," I said.

He smiled.

"You better go anyway," his father advised, pointing at the clock.

"Okay, Dad," Kevin said in a deft imitation of his father's serious Dad Voice.

We managed to not crack up until we had gotten to the street.

Side by side we walked, the laughter dying down as suddenly as it had bubbled up, and then silence settled between us. We got to the corner and waited for the bus, never making eye contact.

six

I SPENT THE whole morning at school not thinking about Kevin. It took all my attention because he was in so many of my classes. I especially tried not to see him when he was walking between classes with Felicity, nodding at something she was saying to him. Felicity was my best friend until third grade. Now she is the center of the Pop-Tarts, who are Pop(ular) and Tart(y)—not really all that tarty, probably, but anyway, that is what me-and-Tess used to call them. They are actually very sweet and very pretty and very boring. Kevin seemed not to notice that last aspect.

But I was too busy smiling at other people and teachers, chatting with George, and pretending to be normal to be bothered by that. I was so distracted that in my planner, during science, I wrote down, "Think of."

No idea what that even meant. Good luck with that home-work.

Then I spent the next two periods wondering how awkward it would be if I asked Kevin for the homework, and whether I subconsciously for the first time ever just didn't write down the assignment *so that* I would have to ask him for it.

Excellent morning of education.

At lunch I considered going out to the bridge where the smokers and stoners hang, but I really didn't have the courage or desire to be alone among a whole gang of kids I don't know at my own school. So, since it was one of those rare late-March days that was both warm and clear and hinting that maybe spring actually would decide to come back to New England, I just went out to the courtyard to eat my lunch. I could listen to music with my new earbuds and watch Jennifer play basketball with George and Kevin and the other sporty kids, and then have somebody to walk in from lunch with.

Also, I was starving, due to the whole didn't-eat-breakfast thing. It truly sucks when your mother is right. I plopped down on the steps and grabbed my sandwich out of my bag. I bit off a massive chunk of it and was just working out how to chew without gagging on such a ginormous quantity of cheese with pickles and mustard on whole wheat, when Tess plopped down beside me.

She hadn't sat down next to me since Darlene's horrible party. I didn't know what to say to her. I had wished this moment into existence, and now I didn't want to blow this chance. The blob of sandwich in my mouth began to swell. If Tess asked me a question or even just said hello, I was going to have to either spit out the blob or swallow it whole, like a boa constrictor with an ill-advisedly large rodent.

I was starting to drool.

Finally, Tess leaned back, her elbows on the step behind us. I dropped the unbitten part of my sandwich onto the brown bag in my lap, and then, with my body blocking her view, I gagged the continent-size hunk of soggy sandwich out of my mouth into my napkin. Retching only slightly, I crumpled it up into a ball and shoved it, along with the rest of the sandwich, into the brown bag, which I jammed between my feet.

I took a deep breath and pretended to be engrossed in watching the basketball game, hoping for the slim chance Tess hadn't noticed the whole near-puking show.

After an awkward silence, she said, "Well, that was pretty."

I smiled without turning my head. "There goes my future as a boa constrictor."

"Doesn't pay well anyway," she said. "In this economy."

I didn't say, *Oh, Tess, are you my friend again?* or, *I miss you!* or, *If you forgive me for kissing Kevin and not telling you until I announced it to everybody, I will be the best friend ever from now on, I promise.*

Or even, *You weren't always so nice to me, either, you know.*

We just sat there, leaning back on our elbows, side by side. When the bell rang, we walked into school together. I had completely forgotten about waiting for Jen, and also about George, Kevin, my missing homework, and my hunger pangs. At my locker, Tess held out her pack of gum to me, and I took a piece just like nothing.

My stomach grumbled with hunger all the rest of the afternoon, or maybe from finally unclenching.

seven

I WAS ON my way through the lobby when George caught me by the shoulders and yanked me back toward him. "You're in my clutches now!" he said, and kissed my hair.

He is such a nice guy. "Hi, George," I said.

"You okay?"

"Yup."

We chatted for a minute about whether the math homework was boring busywork or actually just hard. Then he had to run to band. I watched him go, knowing he would turn and smile at me before he rounded the corner. I waved. Then I turned around and walked home through the woods, looking at the new buds dotting the no-longer-completely-skeletal tree branches. Spring always comes, I was thinking, no matter how frigging unlikely it looks as the snow melts.

I think about the weather when I don't want to think about other stuff, such as whether it is possible to be falling in love with two different guys.

Nobody was home, thankfully, when I got there, so I did my homework (the part I could decipher from my planner) in peace while eating pretty much everything in the fridge, and then went up to my room. I signed onto Facebook. Tess still hadn't re-friended me. I posted on a bunch of people's walls looking for someone who knew what we had to do for science, and then, since nobody had answered—just one superquiet kid I have never actually spoken to "liked" the fact that I had no clue what the homework was—I signed out.

How does a person figure out which boy she likes if she doesn't have a best friend?

No texting Tess. Be cool. Wait, I told myself.

Having nobody to text, I lay down on my bed, my cell phone still and cold as a dead turtle on my stomach as I drifted toward sleep.

I woke up completely discombobulated in the dark. I checked my phone. A message! But not from Tess. A number I didn't recognize, asking me to come in on Wednesday afternoon.

Where?

I could hear people downstairs and wondered when, if ever, I would stop being surprised that Kevin Lazarus and his family were living in my house.

"Charlie!" my mother yelled up the stairs. "We're waiting

for you! Come on down for dinner!"

"Yeah," I answered. "Right. Okay." So I hadn't slept through dinner. Good. I was starving. I jumped up out of bed and started the dash toward the dining room, but then went back to my room to grab my phone. That unfamiliar number, I realized, was probably Anya from Cuppa. *Yes.*

I texted back, *YES.*

"Charlie!" Mom yelled again.

"Coming!"

"We were waiting for you," my mother growled when I got there. She never used to growl at me.

I decided not to look at her, either.

It was possible if things continued this way, I would never make eye contact with another living person the rest of my life.

Out of the blue, Joe chanted, "Too much noise! Too much noise!"

Samantha joined in, and Kevin may have, too, quietly: "Too much noise! Too much noise!" I looked at each of them, despite my recent vow not to, ever, but I mean, what the heck was happening?

My mother crinkled her nose and tilted her head, her code for *Please explain.*

Her husband smiled gently at her, at Samantha, then back at Mom. "Old family joke," he said, winking, and then asked Samantha, "Right?"

Mom smiled like, *Oh, okay,* but I could tell she felt a little left out.

"It's hard to be a new family when the old family has jokes some of us don't get," Joe said. "Sorry." He kissed my mother, on the lips. In front of us.

It is hard to be a new family in so many ways, actually, I was thinking, and then I started wondering when I could slip upstairs and hide in my room, since obviously nobody was about to kiss me and make it better. Hahahaha. As if kissing me ever made anything better.

"It's from this time," Joe started explaining, "when we were living in the city, and these people were marching past our building, protesting something, and we thought . . ."

"No," Sam corrected. "That was 'We want pastries! Pitza-poddle now!' 'Too much noise' is a different story. Remember?"

"It doesn't matter," Kevin said.

"No, I thought, wasn't that the time—"

"Dad," Kevin interrupted. "Please."

"I embarrass him," Joe said to my mother. "Goofy Dad Syndrome."

"Dad!" Kevin slammed his palm against the table, and we all jumped. "If you have to talk, at least SAY something. Don't just spew randomly."

"Touché," Joe said. "So, um, well. Your mother called again today."

"Why?" Samantha asked after a moment of heavy quiet.

"She wanted to tell me that she bought the tickets for you guys to come out to Idaho to visit her over spring break."

They didn't respond at all, just sat there. It was silent except for forks clicking on plates. The weird lack-of-talking lasted way longer than seemed at all normal, during which I had plenty of time to wonder what the hell was going on. Again. It was weirder than the Too Much Noise fiasco that had just passed.

Then, for the Grand Finale (I hoped) of Suppertime Oddness, Joe started quizzing Kevin and Samantha on what they had learned at school that day.

Seriously, my mother and I had passed entire meals, entire months without anything this peculiar going on. I tried to make eye contact with her to be like, *Aren't we in a strange bit here together, you and I?* But she was staring pleasantly down at her plate.

"We have to come up with science fair projects," Kevin was volunteering. "Everybody in ninth grade."

Oh, I thought. *Check. Okay. Thanks.* I hadn't posted my question on his wall, of course. But there he was, giving me the answer to my *What was the science homework?* question anyway.

"Have you considered making a non-Newtonian fluid?" Joe asked me and Kevin.

"It's all I've been thinking about," I answered.

"Charlie," Mom warned.

"Me too," Kevin said, watching Sam. She was holding a string bean between her pointer and thumb, observing it. Then she let go.

"Sam," Joe said. "Don't."

She slid off her chair to retrieve the string bean.

"Is that also called—goop?" my mother asked Joe.

"Yes! Don't tell me you made goop for a science fair project, too?"

"No," Mom said. "Just killed some plants, I think."

"Sam," Joe barked. The string bean was halfway into her mouth. She let go with her skinny fingers but not her teeth, so it hung there limply.

Joe smiled gently. "Don't eat off the floor, sweetheart."

"Five-second rule," Sam said. The string bean, still half-in/half-out, twitched as she spoke.

"That's not . . ." Joe's smile was starting to mold. "That rule does not make one bit of sense."

"Mom says it does," Sam said. "My mom." She then proceeded to slowly chomp the string bean, which disappeared millimeter by millimeter.

We all watched. When she finished, Joe took a deep breath, turned his face away from Samantha's, and shrugged apologetically to my mother. "How was your day, my love?" he asked her.

So much for my appetite. I'd been holding my phone in my lap the whole dinner, but Kevin, I guess, didn't feel like texting under the table right then. Luckily. Because I certainly did not need to be texting with him. Hopefully he had gotten the point and was planning to just ignore me, too.

I slipped my phone into my pocket to clear my plate from the table as soon as it seemed like I could get away without being yelled at.

After a minute, when I was standing in the kitchen checking my phone to make sure it hadn't died, Samantha followed me in, carrying her plate with the silverware and her cup on top. "Where's the broom?" she asked.

"Did something break?"

"No," she said.

"Why do you need a broom, then?"

"To sweep up after dinner. It's my job."

"Oh," I said. "Um . . ." I tried to think of where we kept a broom.

"What's yours?"

"My what?" I asked her, leaving my plate in the sink and opening the hall closet to broom-search. "My broom?"

"Job."

"I, my job? I didn't—I just have an interview." It hit me that I had not yet asked my mother if I could get a job. "I don't actually have a job. Yet."

"After dinner," Samantha patiently explained, beginning to wash off her plate thoroughly before placing it gently in the dishwasher. "What is your job, after dinner?"

"Um, walking the dog."

"There's a dog?" she asked, excited for the first time I'd ever seen. I felt instantly awful. "Where? I didn't know we had a dog!"

"We don't. Sorry."

"So, but you said, your job is walking the dog?"

"If we had one, I meant." My shoulders weighed a thousand

pounds each. "So for now I am off the hook. Is what I meant. Lame joke. Sorry."

"Oh."

"Is Charlie torturing you?" Kevin asked her, coming into the kitchen with his plate stacked similarly with his place-setting stuff. On his way he grabbed the saucepot off the stove, too.

"Not on purpose," I said. I grabbed a pear out of the bowl of fruit that was sitting like a still life on the kitchen counter.

"I wouldn't," Kevin said.

"Wouldn't . . . what?"

"Monday pears," Samantha said. The two of them were both looking at the pear in my hand, which started to feel like a grenade I had just accidentally pulled the pin out of.

"What's wrong with it?" I asked them.

They both shrugged.

"Monday pears?" I asked. "Is that a thing? Or another old family joke?"

Samantha said, "It's a thing, I think."

Kevin shrugged, then went to the sink and started scrubbing the pot. I felt like a geranium plunked down awkwardly in the middle of my own kitchen. I bravely took a bite of the pear. I waited, but nothing happened like instant death or puking. It was just a hard, juiceless pear. No taste, not even poison.

Joe materialized in the kitchen doorway with a broom and dustpan, which he handed to Samantha, and then kissed her on top of her head. She disappeared into the dining room to do her job. I sank onto a kitchen chair and took another hard bite out of the pear. I checked my phone while all the busy elves buzzed around me. No messages except one from George, asking if I wanted to do homework together online.

Sorry too late done already, I texted back.

Grind, he texted, and then a few seconds later, a smiley face. He had probably already finished, too. He was at least as big a grind as me.

Since my phone was just sitting there in my hand, not serving any good purpose, I texted Tess. So much for my plan not to. What I texted was:

So weird here.

Then I went upstairs to try to remember some inside jokes between Mom and me, to be sure to use in front of that other family who lives with us, and fell asleep in my bed until 3:32 a.m.

eight

I FOUND MY phone on the floor beside my bed. No text back from Tess. 3:33 a.m. Do you get to make a wish at 3:33? Tess never used to take more than a minute to text back. I decided not to interpret but instead to focus on the fact that I had been sleeping in my clothes and also that I had to pee.

I yanked off my jeans and T-shirt and bra, dropped all that on the floor, and stomped into my flannel boxers. I started pulling on a big T-shirt, but then I remembered enough about my current life to change my mind. I pulled on a tank top with bra support instead, even as I was swearing to myself I was just going to the bathroom and then back to bed. It was my cute pink tank top, the one Tess had once said looked hot.

I tiptoed to the bathroom in the dark and closed the door. When I sat down on the toilet, it was about four perilous inches lower than normal. I may have shrieked. I came disgustingly close to drowning bottom-first in the toilet, with its seat left up.

With my heart pounding and breath raggedy, I washed my hands extra well. Because, gross. I brushed my teeth fast and hard, then opened the door and gasped.

"Hi," Kevin whispered, his face two inches from mine.

"Jesus," I said.

"No," he answered. "Just Kevin."

I shoved him. His stomach is very flat and firm, I couldn't help noticing. I made a mental note to do a sit-up someday soon. "Well, *Just Kevin*, you left the toilet seat up."

"Sorry," he whispered.

"Okay."

"You smell good," he whispered.

"Oh," I romantically retorted.

"Come 'ere," he whispered, and walked away from me, toward his room, the old guest room.

He stopped in the doorway and waited for me. I tiptoed down the hall and stepped inside.

"Didn't you have to go to the bathroom?"

"No." He closed the door behind me.

Closed it.

My whole body started shivering.

He sat down on his bed.

Not that it ever came up as a rule, but I was fairly sure that I would not be allowed to be in a bedroom alone with a boy in my house, with the door closed, in the middle of the night.

I sat down on his bed, too, but not exactly next to him. He faced me, his right leg triangled on the bed, the left down on the floor. I kept both my feet on the floor. Unsure whether to face him or stay profile, I alternated, as if a superspeed tennis match were being played in front of me. Not Good. I decided to stare at my hands, which were clutching each other in my lap, and to stay silent and still until he made the first move.

"I used to play in here," I blurted immediately after that decision. "Playmobil, and I would make forts, with Tess, pretend we were adventurers, scientists. We decided, me and Tess, I mean, we decided to be epidemiologists for about a month, until her sister, Lena, told us what epidemiologists were." *Can somebody please shut me up?*

He didn't respond, and didn't respond, and still didn't respond. The randomness of that little anecdote filled up Kevin's silent room like noxious fumes. We would be found dead in the morning. The paramedics would nod comfortingly to our perplexed parents. *Must've been that odd epidemiology comment, ma'am, sir. Sorry for your loss.*

So jittery I risked levitation, I popped up and looked around. "You all unpacked?"

"No," he said.

"You choose a science fair project yet?"

"No."

"Me neither. No ideas, even. Other than Fig Newtony goop, I guess. Haha." He didn't laugh. Unable to shut the heck up, I plowed relentlessly on. "Your father suggested . . . Just kidding. Anyway, so, hey, you're going to visit your mom over break?"

"Guess so."

"Is that—you like to visit her?"

"It's okay."

Stop interviewing him! "Oh, you're lucky, then. I hate to visit my dad. His wife is all, like, she thinks she's on a commercial for cereal, you know? And I have a half brother. His name is Alexander, but they call him ABC. Those are his initials. Is why."

"Uh-huh."

I took a deep breath, hoping there was something other than helium in the air, because that's what I felt like I'd been sucking. "Idaho, huh?"

"Yeah."

"Why did she—I mean, how long have your parents been . . ."

"Long time."

"Oh, mine too. Such a long time. I don't even remember mine together, actually."

"I do," he said. "I remember mine."

"Oh." *Urgh, why am I such a freak?* I realized abruptly that I was breathing like I'd just sprinted to the finish line. How to breathe normally? No memory of the technique.

To avoid his intense eyes, I turned away and pretended to look at the stuff on his desk, which was set up where the guest room dresser used to be. I tried to slow myself down—my pulse, my yammering. *Just stay quiet for three breaths, Charlie!* On his desk I saw his open drawing pad, which my mother had bought him for Christmas, and there, on the exposed page, was the weirdest, most beautiful picture I had ever seen.

"What is this?" Oops, only got through the one breath.

"Nothing." He stood up quickly and flipped the pad shut.

"You drew that?"

He stood between me and the desk, with his back to me and his hand heavy on the closed pad.

"Kevin, you drew that?"

His head sagged.

"It's, it's, well, it's beautiful. Let me see it. Come on. Let me see it!" *Oh, good, badger him. Excellent.* How to Win Friends, *by Charlie Collins.*

"No."

I stopped grabbing at the pad but let my fingers linger there, near his. "I don't think I've ever seen colors like that," I whispered. "How did you get those colors?"

"Pastel pencils," he whispered back, much softer. "You wet them."

"It, this is going to sound stupid, because I don't know anything about art, and probably it was supposed to be abstract and I'm too unsophisticated to get it, but it kind of looked like the trees, you know, down by the lake? But not, obviously."

He squinted at me as if I were written in fine print.

"Next to the ugly bush with the prickers?"

51

"No, they didn't."

"Oh. Okay."

"Only to me. And to you."

A few jokes tried to break free of my mouth, like, *Well, maybe we could do a survey,* or, *How many people did you actually ask?* or, *Well, maybe if you used actual tree colors, more people would see that you'd drawn trees,* but my teeth held them in. And I wouldn't want him to change that picture. The trees in it, the trees that I saw just for those few seconds on his pad, looked more like the trees down at the bottom of our hill than the actual trees did. So I just stood there, straight as a parallel line in front of him, not smirking or joking, just there.

"Damn, Charlie," he whispered. "Who *are* you?"

"Um, I don't know."

"I always thought you were just . . . a funny girl. Hot, but silly."

Hot? Really? *SILLY?*

"But the more I get to know you, the more I don't know. . . ."

I said something vaguely like *urghaswdftijkol* and backed a step away.

His eyes, so intensely blue, narrowed slightly. He closed the distance I'd opened up between us and kissed me lightly on the lips. "Maybe we can just *be*," Kevin whispered. His words touched my mouth as breath, blowing across the spot on my lips where his lips had just pressed. "It doesn't have to be complicated. Just find a cool space together. No rules, no labels, we can keep it undefined even, no complications at all. Just . . ."

"A cool space."

His face was nearing mine again, his blue eyes closing as he approached, my eyes closing, too. I could feel my mouth moving to meet his, the warmth of his lips on mine. . . .

I stepped back. "No," I said.

"No?" He blinked his sleepy eyes open.

"No. I'm sorry."

"Because of George?"

"Yeah."

"But you said you and George aren't even going out."

"Officially."

"So . . ."

"But I like him."

Kevin stepped back and said, "Oh."

"But not just George. I also like . . ."

"Who else?"

"Clarity," I said, shaking my head. "I'm sorry, but I do. Maybe that's uncool, but there it is. Things were so much easier before it got all murky."

"Murky."

"Yes," I said. "I like things to be defined. I don't want to sneak around. It's not fair to George, or to you or me, either. Also, I mean, we did that, and—look how it turned out."

"How is what we do any of anybody's business? Especially if you're not officially . . ."

"Kevin."

"Look, if you don't like me, that's fine. Tell me. If you like George better than me, just say so and I will leave you alone, I swear."

I stood there in front of him, not answering. Not knowing the answer.

His eyes searched mine.

"*Keep it undefined*," I said instead of answering. "What does that even mean, *undefined*?"

He smirked.

"What?"

"You want me to define *undefined*."

I smirked back.

"And you didn't answer."

My smirk melted away.

"You do like me," he said.

"I'm trying not to."

"How's that going?"

"Not so well, right now," I admitted.

"Good."

"Kevin. It's just—a bad idea," I whispered. "I mean, complicated doesn't begin . . ."

"Absolutely." He stepped toward me again.

"Gotta go," I said, bolting from his room. I needed to get out of there. Not need like sometimes I need gum if I've eaten a loaf of garlic bread, but need like air, if a pillow is being shoved onto your face.

nine

"CHARLIE!"

"Oh! Hi, George." He had come up behind me at my locker. I pulled the earbuds he'd bought me out of my ears. "What's up?"

"Want to go sit on the upper field for lunch?"

"Uh . . ."

"She can't," Tess interrupted, coming around the corner.

"I can't," I agreed.

"She promised to hang with me," Tess explained.

George looked back and forth between us. "Hell froze over? Pigs flew?"

"Haha," Tess said, and grabbed my arm. "Come on, Charlie."

We walked down the hall to the back doors, arms linked.

Out on the steps, we sat right next to each other, shoulders occasionally bumping, like old times.

"He's a great guy," I said in between purposely tiny bites of sandwich. "George."

"The best," Tess agreed.

"So why did you—"

"You just looked like you wanted to be rescued."

I chewed and thought. "I guess." We watched Jen and the boys shoot hoops.

"You should break up with him."

"We're not officially going out."

"Break up unofficially, then. It's mean to string him along. He loves you, but you don't love him."

I groaned. "How do you know?"

"I know you. I can tell. So, trust me. Like a Band-Aid— fast, ouch, done."

"You think?" I asked.

She smiled. "Sometimes, but it gives my brain a cramp, so I have to stop."

"I hate ripping off Band-Aids."

"Who doesn't? Still." She looked me straight in the eye, my mirror image with slightly finer features and longer hair. "You were right, what you said."

"I was? When?"

"At Darlene's party."

That I kissed Kevin? "What—which—why . . ."

"You said it was always like you came in second place," Tess explained. "It's true. I wanted to deny it, but you were right. And that I used you. And maybe I used Kevin, too. I knew how much you both liked me and maybe took advantage of that."

"Oh."

"You were right, and I was blind to all that. Or maybe just didn't want to know. But, whatever. I'm over it. You and Kevin kind of used each other to get back at me. That's all it ever was between you. I get that now."

I had no words.

"Also . . ."

I turned to look at her again. Her eyes were even more sparkly than usual. She blinked twice, swallowed, cleared her throat. Her pretty mouth curved down into a frown as she whispered, "I miss you."

"I miss you, too, Tess."

"So, we rescue each other." She sniffed once, hard, and forced a brave smile.

"We . . ."

"I rescue you from lunch with your boyfriend, who loves you, and you rescue me from lunch with the Pop-Tarts, who are so damn boring with all their giggling and backhanded compliments, I want to put a fork through my eye."

I laughed. Tess laughed. And right then, the sun came out from behind a cloud and shined down hard on us. "Wow," I said. "No subtlety at all, huh, sun?"

"If you were made of explosions," Tess said, "you'd be unsubtle, too."

"You mean I'm not made of explosions?"

"Good point. We're both made of explosions, too, aren't we? Explains a lot."

I tossed my lunch garbage toward the trash can, and for the first time in my life, it went in. Deciding to take it all as a good omen, I leaned my shoulder against Tess's. She leaned back.

"So it's weird, living with Kevin?" she asked.

"Weird doesn't begin to cover it."

She laughed her wicked laugh, and all felt right with the world. Mostly.

ten

BECAUSE I AM a wimp, I did not launch into my speech until after we got our ice-cream cones. When we sat on the bench together, George put his arm on the bench behind me. My ice cream started to drip onto my fingers.

At least I paid for the cones, was my pathetic self-commiseration.

Though even then, I did say okay, that he could buy next time. Which made starting the conversation that much worse. I stalled by concentrating on my ice cream.

He licked around the bottom of his scoop to keep any of his Cookie Dough Dynamo from dripping, then asked, "How's life in the new blended family?"

"Um, I, it, what? Good, I guess."

"What's wrong, Charlie? You seem . . . weird."

"I am weird."

"True, but usually in a good way. Hey, did Tess say something mean again?"

"No," I said. "We're actually, things are better."

"Good," he said. "Just be careful."

"Of what?"

"In general."

"Of falling in a hole? Stepping in poop? What are you talking about, George? Be careful in general? What the heck kind of thing is that to say to a person?" I was shrieking. It was unsettling us both.

"Of Tess," he said quietly.

"She's my BEST FRIEND."

"Oh . . . kay," he said, and we both intensely ate our ice cream for a moment.

"Sorry," I said without looking at him. We licked our cones in silence for a minute, until I took a deep breath and said, "I don't even know how to say this and not be more of a jerk than I already am."

"Just say it," he whispered.

"You are the nicest guy in the world."

"Oh. Really? That's the—oh." He stood up and tossed his half-eaten ice-cream cone into the trash can beside the bench. He wiped his hands clean on his napkin and then tossed that into the can, too, before sitting back down. This time, his arm wasn't around me. "Fine, go ahead."

I took a deep breath and launched into my prepared

comments. My notes, jotted down during social studies, were in my bag, but I decided against pulling them out and went from memory instead. "You said, at my mother's wedding, that the one I need to forgive, about the whole mess I created with Tess and Kevin and all that, was myself."

"Uh-huh," he said without looking up from his clasped hands, which were between his wide-spread knees. "I did. I said that. It's true, by the way."

"Well, maybe you're right. I don't know." I watched my ice cream melt down over the cone and drip onto the sidewalk between my sneakers. First really warm spring day, and this is how I was spending it.

"I am right," he said. "Go on."

"Yeah. Or maybe, like my father loves to tell me, I am too quick to let myself off the hook. I don't know."

"Your father is a tool. Sorry, just saying."

"That's okay. Thanks, actually. But anyway, what I need, I think, is to sort some stuff out. For myself."

"Fine."

"But, I can't do it, I can't figure out why I did what I did and how to make up for it—to Tess, or to Kevin, even to you . . ."

"You have nothing to make up to me, Charlie. I told you. Leave me out of your self-flagellation. I wasn't going out with you at the time of the Great Transgression."

"Stop calling it that, George, seriously," I said. "Besides. Still."

"No," he said, sounding for the first time ever a little angry at me. "Really, leave me out of that part. You don't owe me any apologies or reparations or whatever you think you owe everybody. And I am pretty sure you don't owe Kevin an apology, either. No way. So, what? You were a jerk? Okay, fine, maybe you were. Whatever. Everybody's a jerk at some point. Get over it."

"I was a very large jerk," I pointed out.

"Now we're just haggling about size," he said.

"What?"

"Never mind," he muttered. "Go on. You were in the middle of breaking up with me."

"Oh, George."

"I never asked you out, by the way. Just saying. But still. Go ahead."

"See? This is what I mean. I can't figure all this out if I'm your sort-of unofficial girlfriend, because you are way too nice and funny and it confuses me."

"Sorry," he said. "I'll work on being less nice, for future unofficial girlfriends."

"I know you think you're doing the moral thing by sticking by me . . ."

"Yeah, that's why I've stuck with you. Making a moral point. If I get a hundred moral points, I can trade them in for valuable merchandise."

"George."

"Toasters, pencil sharpeners, dusting cloths . . ."

"George!"

"Go on. I've stuck with you because . . . ?"

"Because you are very, I don't know, gallant."

"Gallant? Really? Gallant? Like a knight?"

"Yes. And I've appreciated it, this whole time, so much, but I just, I have to ask you to stop. Okay? Please understand."

He raised his eyebrows and opened his mouth to say something, but stopped before any words came out. We sat there silent for a minute or three, both miserable.

"I just, I need to be alone for a while," I said. "To be independent, as you once said I was, but you were wrong then, or at least maybe just . . . optimistic."

"Okay."

"This is my mess, so I have to sleep in it. Or whatever."

"Yeah, or, are you dumping me because now you've suddenly got Tess back? So you don't need me?"

"George, no." The ice cream was gurgling around in my clenched stomach. "That's not it."

"Or maybe," he said, "you're giving me the boot because you're hot for Kevin Lazarus."

"No!" Wow, that was loud. "No, George. I swear that's not why."

He didn't say anything, so I forced myself to turn and look at him.

"I mean, I'm not. George, come on. Why are you being so mean suddenly?"

He shrugged. "Somebody really smart who I used to love

suggested I should be less nice. Thanks for the ice cream."

He used to love me?

He stood up, so I did, too. My hands were sticky with radioactive-looking melted mint chip ice cream.

"Hey, George . . . ," I said, launching into the conclusion I'd written in the margin of my notebook earlier in the day. "I just, I hope you will know someday that this is a new leaf for me, my first step in trying to do the right thing and be a good friend."

"It is what it is," George said, and started to walk away. He turned around after about twenty steps and grinned his lopsided grin at me. "Is it bad that I'm feeling happy you paid for the ice cream?"

I smiled back. "No," I answered. "Not at all."

eleven

A CAR PULLED into the driveway. I froze at the window in Samantha's room, where I was hiding while watching Kevin and his friends throw a football around our yard. The car door slammed. By the time Samantha's light footsteps approached the second floor, I was in my room, pretending to read, casually, on my bed.

That lasted about a minute before I peeked out into the hallway. Samantha was flopped against the wall like an abandoned stuffed animal.

"You okay?"

"Mmmm," she said, her eyes closed but fluttering under her eyelids.

"Long day?" I asked. "Playdate?"

She reluctantly opened her eyes to slits. "I get worn out by people sometimes."

"Me too," I admitted.

Her eyes closed again.

"Maybe you should drink some water."

"I'm watching the colors," she said slowly.

"The colors."

"Funny, huh?"

Kind of funny, I thought. Funny weird. "Uh . . ."

"I have too many and Kevin has too few."

"Too few . . . what?" I asked.

"Colors."

"Colors?"

She didn't respond. So I had nothing to echo.

I went to the bathroom and got us each a paper cup of cool water to drink, and sat down next to her. The dispenser of Dixie cups was yet another new addition in my house—but kind of a fun one. Little bitty cups for water, any time you wanted some. I downed my shot of water and considered whether I should leave Sam alone, or call her dad to come upstairs to deal with this.

After a few minutes, Sam took a tiny sip, then stood up. "Do you mind if I go read now?" she asked me.

"Not at all."

"Thank you for the water." She took another microsip.

I watched her wander to her room and close her door. I stayed there in the hall until my butt fell asleep, then headed down to the kitchen in search of a snack. I hadn't finished my ice cream, I internally negotiated.

I was eating another hard pear in front of the open fridge when the gang of boys came in. They all said stuff to me like *Hey* and *How's it going.* They joked about how clumsy Brad was, how he couldn't catch a cold, never mind a ball, not seeming weirded out at all to have me there, added to the mix, as they chugged water out of glasses Mom and I had bought three years ago. They all nodded a lot, bobbleheadishly. I know girls are the ones who supposedly like to get along, and boys fight—but, it turns out, not so much.

"Hot out," Kevin said.

"Practically a heat wave," Tariq joked.

"Hot enough to cook a chicken," Brad added.

Then they all cracked up, so I did, too, and then they were shuffling out, saying good-bye and *See ya* and *Take it easy* and *Cook-a-chicken hot.*

As he passed me, Kevin's hand traced a line across my back, about five inches north of the top of my jeans.

It felt like lightning.

He walked out with his friends, but his touch stayed there, with me.

For dinner, Mom made refrigerator salad with the dregs of the wedding leftovers. It was good, one of my favorite kinds of dinner, in fact, but it was hard to fully enjoy with Joe practically moaning about how delicious it all was. Dude, it's leftovers chopped up. I actually liked the guy a little when he and Mom were dating, but it's like perfume—a bit is fine, nice, even; too much and your eyes water.

"We have a ton of homework," Kevin said in an oddly chipper voice as we cleared the table. "We should . . ."

"Oh, okay," Joe said. "Hit the books. I'll do the scrub-up tonight."

"Um, okay," I said. On the stairs, going up to our rooms, Kevin bumped me with his shoulder.

"Cool dishwashing dodge," I said.

"I'm awesome."

"If you do say so yourself." I turned my face away because I could feel myself staring at his red, red lips, and also feeling tempted to tell him I'd broken up with George. Which was none of his business and had nothing to do with him. So there was no reason to tell him.

"You want to come in?" he asked at his door. "We could, you know . . ."

I raised my eyebrows.

"Read *Hamlet* together. What were you thinking of?"

I laughed. He does make me laugh.

"Because, if you had other ideas . . . ?"

I shoved him into his room but stayed in the hall and said, "Rain check."

"Yeah?"

"No," I said, and walked away, toward my room, feeling him watching me.

Behind me, Kevin groaned like he was in delicious pain.

I closed my door but not totally.

There was no way I could settle down enough to read

about Hamlet's scheming stepfather and how awkward it was for Hamlet to deal with a blended family. Uh, no.

I put in my new earbuds to block out the world and listen to some show tunes while doing math, but that felt really crappy. I did love those earbuds—which were such a thoughtful gift, and maybe I had made a huge, inexplicable, unfixable error by dumping George—but now I kind of had no moral right to use them. Also, it is very hard to focus on equations with *Next to Normal* blasting in your ears.

Is *everything* about weird family dynamics?

I took out the earbuds, hid them under my pillow, and opened my science notebook to today's page. It was blank other than "Science Fair Project Proposal" and my name. Nothing else appeared magically under it, so I gave up on that and texted Tess:

> *today at lunch I was happier than I have been*
> *since the night I wrecked everything*
> *or maybe even before that*

Over the next half hour of not coming up with any decent science fair ideas, I checked my phone about eighty times. Nothing. I decided to hate myself for texting her such unsubtle, needy, clingy crap and then checked Facebook, in case she was on and wanted to chat. Nope. She was still listed as one of Felicity's many sisters, and Felicity as one of hers. I had no siblings. Urgh. I signed out and closed my computer. Then I opened it again and shut it off. Better. I closed it, tucked it into my bag, buckled it up, and shoved the whole thing under my bed. I wanted to make it impossible to casually stalk Tess's page or request that she be my sister, too.

Why was she not texting me back?

I finished my math and moved on to force myself through the *Hamlet* reading. I was annotating *Why would Ophelia put up with that crap from him, even if he is a prince* when I almost fell off my bed. I thought it might be an earthquake, but no, it was my phone buzzing.

The text from Tess, which I read until I had it memorized and then a few times more, seemed more poetic to me than anything ol' Willy Shakes had written in the book in my other hand:

> *ok good.*
> *hey, i love you okay?*
> *and i forgive you and stuff*
> *obviously*
> *and dont feel bad*
> *if you still do*
> *okay . . . thats probs it*
> *xoxo*

I waited until I had finished doing the *Hamlet* reading before I allowed myself to text back:

> *Thanks, Tess. U r the bessssttttt.*

She texted back a winking face, and so we went back and

forth making faces out of numbers and signs for a while in between finishing our homework, and parsing what George had said and whether I had handled breaking up with him well. She said I just had to move on, because if you aren't in love with a boy, you shouldn't string him along.

I guess u r right, I texted her.

She wrote back immediately, *I am always right u no that.*

I went with emoticons for a response. Because what else could I say? I was just feeling bad. Especially because I had the earbuds in again, so I could listen to music while we texted some more, until Tess wrote that her mom was doing her nightly prowl to make sure she and her sisters were off their phones, so she had to flop down and fake sleep.

I said I would do the same, in solidarity, even though she and I both knew that my mother didn't do a nightly prowl.

I was surprised when my phone buzzed again, but when I saw the text was from Kevin, I was even more surprised. He'd written:

Is it true you broke up w George?

I texted back *yes* and waited. Nothing else happened. No follow-up questions, no emoticons, no response.

Usually I am asleep within a minute of head-on-pillow, so it was weird to lie there for so long, earbuds tossed across my room, straining to hear the breathing of the boy just seven steps down the hall.

twelve

TESS WAS WAITING at my locker when I got to school. As I dropped my math textbook in and fished out my slightly crushed spiral notebooks, Tess told me that she had woken up with a brilliant idea to cheer me up from the doldrums of having dumped George. I should have a sleepover party Saturday night and we could all drive Kevin nuts, or maybe he could invite some boys over and it would effectively be a coed sleepover. Because even though Kevin is a jerk-slut, some of his friends are seriously getting hot lately.

"Really?" I asked. "Like which?"

Right then, Jennifer and Brad walked past us, chatting. I appraised Brad from my position on the floor. Not bad, it was true. In middle school, he was such a pudgeball.

"When did that even happen?" I asked Tess.

"Exactly."

"Are he and Jennifer going out?"

Tess shrugged. I promised I would ask my mom about the party.

At lunchtime, Tess grabbed me by the arm and brought me to the cafeteria table where she's been sitting with Darlene, Felicity, and Felicity's constant shadow, Paige. Tess told them I was going to have a sleepover on Saturday, and they all immediately started planning which boys we should get Kevin to invite. I tried to explain that I wasn't even sure the party was happening, but Tess assured everybody that my mom never said no.

"Is that true?" I asked. "Maybe I just don't ask for anything."

"Guess it's time to start," Tess suggested.

"Your mom really is nice," Felicity said. "And cool. Like, not overinvolved in your life. My mom wants to know every little detail of mine. She's not a helicopter mom. She's, like, an umbrella. A hat. She's a hat mom."

"Not mine," Darlene said. "My mom said last night she doesn't want to hear one more thing about my life."

"Ooo. Did you get another note home?" Paige asked in her squeaky voice.

"Yeah, D-minus in science. My mom says she's changing my name, legally, to Constant Crisis."

"Can she actually do that?" Paige asked, her blue eyes huge and round with horror.

"Till I'm eighteen, supposedly," Darlene said. "So, anyway, yeah, Charlie—you're lucky your mom is cool."

"Or doesn't know about the name-changing thing," I said.

"Charlie broke up with George," Tess said, getting out her notebook to write a list of boys I should tell Kevin to invite. "So he's out. Too awkward."

"Aw, really?" Felicity asked. "What happened?"

I shrugged. "It just didn't work out."

"Too bad," she said. "You guys were a really cute couple."

"Thanks," I said, and slumped like a single parenthesis on the hard bench.

By the time I left school, I was exhausted. Also, my science project was probably going to be rejected, even though I thought it was a pretty interesting scientific question, one a lot more worthy of investigation than how to make something also known as goop.

I walked straight to Cuppa and got there before four. I pressed my face against the glass from the outside, trying to see who was in there, what was going on. *Be prepared*, I thought, despite my lack of Boy Scout history.

The window was cool against my forehead, but other than that, I didn't learn much. I stood there squinting, though, determined to figure out something. The level of not knowing in my life had me kind of jittery even before taking in the coffee fumes.

When I mustered the courage to walk through the door, I saw Anya, behind the counter, waving at me as if I were approaching across a field of hay instead of just past the four or five tables between us. "Charlie!" she shouted.

Everybody turned in their seats and stared at me. Ah, my absolute-tippy-top-favorite of all pastimes: being looked at. I backed sideways a few steps, and my sneaker crunched down on something.

Beside me, someone sighed. "Oh, great."

"Hi, Penelope!" Penelope was a senior. She had edited my few failed attempts at writing for the school newspaper earlier in the year, before I quit.

"I just swept all that," she said, pointing down at the dust/crumb pile I'd managed to scatter.

"Oh," I said. "I didn't, um . . . You work here?"

She sighed. "Can you just . . . Mom?"

Anya turned her head to look over her shoulder from the cappuccino machine. "Come on back, Charlie!"

"Anya is your mom?"

"So?"

"That's so cool."

I stepped to the side as Penelope sighed behind me. I headed to the counter, past a table of women with strollers, and another of three senior girls I knew by sight but not name, who all had their cell phones out while they chatted and laughed.

Anya handed me an apron. "So there are a bunch of people who want the job, and I can only hire one, so I decided we'll do a trial run for each of you and see how it goes."

"Fair enough," I said, tying the apron tightly around my waist in what I hoped was a winning style.

"Do you know how to use the espresso maker?" she asked.

"Um."

"The frother?"

"I'm a fast learner."

"Okay. Well, let's start at the beginning. How do you like your coffee?"

Wow, this was going well. I should just take off the apron and not waste her time. "I actually don't drink coffee."

"You don't." More of a statement than a question.

"Well, no. Not really."

"But you want to work at a coffee bar."

"Yes."

"You like cleaning counters?"

"Love it," I said.

She nodded, then pointed at the huge stainless steel machine beside us. "This is the Big Man. Penelope will show you how to use it, or you can ask Toby. He'll be in later, and he's a genius. Has a way with machines. There's a surprising amount of machine work, in the café business."

"Uh-oh," I said.

"Problem?"

"No," I said. "Though, I can barely staple."

Anya laughed one *ha*. "Get tutored by Toby, then, for sure. You and Penelope are friends from school?"

"Well," I said, "I was on newspaper. Briefly. Last year."

"Ah, newspaper," Anya replied, as if that foretold some fortune about me.

"I quit."

"The hours are rough," she empathized, handing me a sponge.

"Oh no," I said. "I don't mind long hours. That's not—"

"It wasn't a trap," she said.

I followed her back into the storeroom.

"I quit in protest," I told her, tilting my head to take in the sight of the high shelves, stacked with teetering boxes, all around us. It felt like we'd fallen into a deep, narrow trench.

"You know how to make tea?"

"Sure." I shrugged. "Cup, tea bag, hot water?"

"No. Gross. Never say or do that again."

"Okay." I was obviously acing this tryout. Unless the other applicants actually murdered a customer during their audition, they had little to fear, clearly.

"I'll teach you, and it will change your life."

"Best offer I've had all year," I said truthfully.

"What were you protesting?" Anya asked, handing me a bulky but surprisingly light cardboard box.

"Protesting?"

"When you quit newspaper."

"Oh. Everything, I guess. First Amendment rights. Oppression. A blue-eyed boy going out with my best friend."

"Ah." She put another three boxes on top. "Good causes."

"Just kidding," I said, following her out through the swinging door despite not being able to see anything over the boxes. "About the boy. That was a joke. Penelope will tell you I have a bad sense of humor."

"No worries." Anya took the top box off the stack in my arms and plopped it onto the counter. "I will teach you to make a good pot of tea. And the blue-eyed boy stays our secret. You want to try taking your first order?"

She pointed with her thumb toward the counter, where Tess was standing with Darlene, Felicity, and Paige. They hadn't mentioned to me that they were coming here after school. I hadn't seen any of them after the last bell. But beyond that, it was all too freaking likely that they had just heard Anya tell me the blue-eyed boy would stay a secret.

As if there could be any mystery who the blue-eyed boy might be.

The stomach-clenching cramps I thought had healed up like an old paper cut were back in force.

"Hi," Tess said. "You *work* here?"

"Probably not," I said. "What can I get you?"

"Seriously?" Darlene asked. "Since when?"

"Now," I said. "Five minutes ago. I just—"

"Cookies-and-cream mocha whip," Tess said.

"Oooh, that sounds good," Darlene said. "Me too. With extra whip?"

Paige frowned nervously at Felicity, her pouty lips curved disappointedly despite their glittery gloss, and whined, "Will you share one with me, Felicity? I'm obese."

Felicity rolled her eyes at me, and I couldn't help smiling in response. Paige is about as obese as a stick. Felicity planted a long-fingered hand on the hip of her dark jeans and considered.

"Okay," Felicity told the anxiously panting Paige, who grinned like a good puppy. "Iced pomegranate green tea, though," she added.

Paige's face sank for a millisecond, then rebounded. You don't say no to Felicity. "Great," Paige squeaked. "Pomegranate green tea! Perfect! I love iced pomegranate green tea! Good idea! Yummy!"

Felicity shook her head microscopically at that, like, *You see what I have to deal with? Save me!* But what she said, in her low voice, was, "A skinny, extra-cold iced pomegranate green tea, and an extra cup."

"Okay," I said, and added perkily, "Coming right up!"

I think Tess may have swallowed a chuckle. But maybe not. She was mad I hadn't told her about possibly getting a job, I knew. I had meant to. If she didn't want me to have the job, that was fine with me, really. I'd rather hang out with her. I obviously was not going to get chosen for it anyway.

"So," Felicity said, leaning across the counter toward me. "Is everything set for Saturday night?"

"Oh," I said. "I haven't asked yet."

"Well, definitely text me later, okay?" Felicity asked. "That would just be so extreme."

"Yeah," Paige said. "Completely extreme."

"Best sleepover ev-ah!" Darlene said, loud enough to make everybody in Cuppa look over at her.

"Okay," I said as Anya handed back their change and then went to finish up their drinks. "I'll see what I can do."

"Congratulations," Tess said. "On your job."

"Thank you," I whispered, hoping nobody else heard the crack in my voice. "It isn't—I don't . . ."

The four of them sat, giggling, at the table Tess and I had picked out, until they finished and waved good-bye.

Meanwhile, I learned how not to wipe the counter, how not to clean the stainless steel, and how not to steam the milk. I burned myself twice on the frother and once with the espresso machine. I learned that most of the chain coffee places use about seven grams of coffee for a two-ounce shot, and those little espresso pods are filled with five grams—but at Cuppa, we tamp down twenty grams. Twenty. "So," I said, showing off that fast-learning skill of mine. "Twenty is way more than seven. Like, thirteen more. Grams."

"Mmm," Anya said. "And we pull it short."

"Obviously."

"Less water. More concentrated." She showed me. I managed to not say that it looked like mud or worse. I just handed the tiny cup to the skinny hipster across the counter, who was reading a thin paperback by Italo Calvino.

Penelope told me to take the trash out. When I lifted the bag, I must have scraped it against something sharp, because within a second, there was garbage all over everything, including my make-a-good-impression shirt. The skinny hipster peered at me condescendingly through his funky glasses as he sipped from that little thimble of poo while I cleaned up all the trash.

Penelope sighed, pointing at the stain my garbage fiasco had left on the wood floor. She gave me a rag to scrub it with. I was so mortified to have made such a mess I was almost happy to do the scrubbing, down there like Cinderella, so at least I could get away from Mr. Too-Cool-to-Not-Be-in-Brooklyn, and also when Anya emerged from the bathroom, I wouldn't have to make eye contact.

"That's enough of that," Anya said. "Want to take one more order before you go?"

"Sure," I said. "Why not."

"Wash hands," she whispered to me, then smiled at the waiting customer. "Just one moment, please."

"We're in a rush," the customer answered.

I dried my hands and asked, "May I help you?"

A gym-hard mom wearing lululemon, a ponytail, and a weary expression stood waiting at the counter, her oversize Birkin bag looped over one arm and her dreary, slumpy daughter behind the other.

"Give me a small, skinny latte," she ordered. "Cecile? Hurry up. Your math tutor will be there in half an hour."

Behind me, Penelope started making the small, skinny latte. I smiled encouragingly at the girl. She had a band of pimples across her forehead and a mouth full of braces.

"Cecile, now," her mother said, tapping away at her phone.

"Um, I'll have a Coke?"

"A Coke?" the mom asked without lifting her eyes from the tiny screen in front of her. "Really, Cecile?"

Poor Cecile sank farther into her shoulders. She was becoming a tortoise right there in front of us.

"She'll have a *Diet* Coke," the mom said to me, still clicking away with her thumbs.

"I hate Diet Coke," Cecile muttered.

Her mother, through gritted teeth, replied, "You have a muffin-top hanging over your jeans, Cecile. And we are not going up a size again. A Coke. She will have a Diet Coke. Quickly, please."

I was on a trial at this job. The customer is always right—I knew that from the sign in the supermarket, for goodness' sake. On the other hand, I had already pretty well blown it. So although Anya was watching me, evaluating me, there was no way I could serve that girl a Diet Coke. Even though I knew it was the right thing to do, I couldn't.

As Penelope handed over the mom's small, skinny latte, I took a large cup, scooped in some ice, and, under the counter, filled it with regular Coke. Filled it to the rim. Then I placed a top on it and handed it to the girl, with a straw. I kept my eyes down, waiting to be told to get my butt out of there, or maybe to be physically tossed out on it, as my dad would say I should be.

The mom was holding out her credit card impatiently. As Anya took it, thanking her, she said to the girl, "You know what? Give that Diet Coke a sip, will you? The machine has been acting up a bit. Make sure the Diet Coke came out okay?"

My face snapped up to Anya's. She'd obviously seen what I'd done.

"I'm sure it's fine," the mom said. "Did it go through?"

Cecile unwrapped the straw, stuck it through the hole in her cup.

"Almost," Anya said, taking her time with the credit card machine, her expression calmly neutral. "Is the Diet Coke fine?"

Cecile's eyes lifted slowly as the sugary drink filled her mouth. She looked from me to Anya and back again. Without stopping her sipping, she nodded. She drained a quarter of the cup before Anya said, "Let Charlie here top that off for you. On the house."

The mom groaned. I grabbed the cup and refilled it with real Coke. Only then did Anya hand over the receipt.

"Have a great day," I said as they left.

"You're hired," Anya said to me after the door closed behind them.

thirteen

I WAS LYING awake in the dark of my room, pondering the eternal existential question that has tortured generations of philosophers: What is there to do at 3:47 a.m. other than go in search of cookies?

Nothing, I answered myself and the ghost-philosophers, honestly.

I tiptoed past the bedroom doors, noticing that Mom's, uniquely, was closed all the way. I clenched my mind against that observation and skulked down the stairs.

She had said yes to my having a sleepover Saturday, at least. Even though she was disappointed I hadn't told her about the job at Cuppa until I came home from my tryout, she said she was proud of me for taking it on. She added that if I found it was interfering with homework, I had to quit. And she suggested maybe I should call my father and discuss it with him, too, but she didn't push it when I said, *Yeah, maybe later.* She was being so damn reasonable, I couldn't even argue.

I got all my homework done before Joe finished quizzing his kids, and slipped into bed behind my closed door before Kevin even came upstairs. Tess hadn't answered my texts all night. When I woke up with a jolt at 3:41, I thought maybe she'd just texted back, finally, but no.

My own fault, again. I know that she hates when I keep something from her, anything, and then there I was, behind the counter at Cuppa. Her supposed best friend. Urgh. Why am I such a bad best friend, when it's the only thing I really even want to be good at? I broke up with George as soon as she told me I should; shouldn't that count for something? I knew I should have told her about Cuppa, about my tryout. Was I scared she'd try out, too, and get the job instead of me? I didn't think so. But how was I supposed to explain when she wasn't even responding to my texts? Maybe she was just finally done with me now?

Ahh. A plastic bag full of leftover brunch cookies sat waiting for me on the counter. I grabbed it and then my fleece off the hook, and headed for the deck. I figured I could eat my cookies and not think while watching the lake emerge from the night as the sky brightened, all by my piranha self.

That is why I almost screamed when I stepped out onto the deck and saw Kevin sitting at the table.

"What are you, why, whoa," I intelligently commented.

Kevin slammed his pad shut and stood up before I could get a good look at what was on it. All I saw was a lot of smudgy lines in weirdly psychedelic colors.

He looked pretty startled to see me, too.

We faced off there, him with his pad, me with my bag o' cookies. Ready to . . . what? Duel?

"Hi," he said.

"You couldn't sleep?" I managed in a whisper.

"No," he whispered back.

"Me neither."

We stood there, for a silent minute.

"I'm not great at sleeping," he said. "You either?"

Usually I am a champion sleeper; it is my best sport. I might go to the Olympics in sleeping. But instead of bragging about that, I whispered, "I like it out here, in the night."

"It's nice," he whispered back.

After another silent-except-for-crickets minute, I let a "Yeah" float out.

"You brought cookies," he said.

"Well, I can't draw, so . . ."

His cheeks burned red as he fingered his pad. He didn't say anything.

"Just kidding. I mean, not about that I can't draw, because I can't, truly, don't even doodle in math class, but I just, you look like I caught you doing something embarrassing, so I just thought, well, a joke will diffuse the—obviously, though, it didn't! More trees? Are you drawing?" I ran out of breath, thankfully, so I stopped talking.

He shrugged.

"Can I see this one?"

"No."

"Why not? Is it for me?" Cringe. Die.

"I don't—show people. Anybody."

"Fine, that's fine. Sure."

Impasse. Okeydokey, then.

After another horrid moment of silence, Kevin said, "I'm color-blind."

"Really?" I put down the bag of cookies on the table beside his closed pad. "Color-blind?"

"Pretty pathetic, for someone who wants to be an artist, huh?"

"Actually," I said, "I think it's kind of cool."

"You do?"

"Well, to see things differently from everybody else? Yeah."

He shook his head. "It's not—I never thought of it that way."

"You want to be an artist?"

"Yeah. Stupid, right? Everybody wants to be an artist, every little kid."

"I don't," I whispered. "I never did. Maybe only artists think that, when they're little."

"What do you want to be?"

I shrugged, trying to think of a goal other than kissing or not kissing him. Save the world from evil? Cure cancer? Win

Tess back? Invent a calorie-burning cookie?

"When you were little," he persisted. "What did you want to be?"

I smiled. "A teenager."

"Most likely to succeed."

"Talk about a stupid wish, huh?"

"Not as much fun as you'd imagined?" He kept his lake-blue eyes latched on to mine, though his head was ducked down.

"It has its moments," I whispered.

"Mmmm," he answered. His smile, that slow, sexy one, spread his mouth and revealed his white teeth. With no choice in the matter, I stood watching. He watched me back.

A shiver shook my body. I wrapped my arms around myself.

He stepped toward me, closer, closer, stopping my thoughts dead. Inches from me, centimeters, he whispered, "Chuck."

We stared at each other, and for once I didn't fill the silence with inane babbles. Just breath.

"I don't think . . . ," I finally whispered.

"Good," he said. "Don't think."

"No," I whispered. "I mean . . ."

"Shhh."

"This is probably a very bad idea, us being out here like this, together in the middle . . ."

"Very bad," he echoed.

"Yes, for so many reasons, so we should . . ."

"Shhh. Can I kiss you?" he asked, his face so close to mine I could feel the heat from it on my cheeks. "I really want to kiss you."

I don't think so.

Not a good idea.

What if our parents walk out here right now?

What if your sister sleepwalks?

I'm not even sure if I actually like you.

Kissing you outside that other time practically wrecked my life.

Who are you to me?

We shouldn't.

"Yes," I said.

He smiled a millimeter and then tipped his head toward mine, his eyes closing.

We met in the middle, our lips touching lightly, so lightly you could barely qualify it as a kiss, so lightly there might have remained a molecule of air between my mouth and his, until, after a moment, there wasn't even that, and then, just as soon, there was, again, the movement as imperceptible as it was unwilled.

We looked at each other, with questions in our eyes. And then I lifted my hands and threaded my fingers into his hair and pulled his mouth to mine.

We breathed each other, kisses upon kisses—faster and harder, more intense—then slower, soft, tender. Soon we were pressing tight against each other and then soft again, a rhythm like unheard music—on and on it played . . . until the trees began to clarify themselves out of the darkness and then, blinking, we let the air fill in the space between us again.

Our lips, a bit bruised and swollen, smiled a little. There was nothing to say, no pretending this was just a slightly flirty *good night* between two not-quite-friends who happen to live together. We both knew we had to get inside, in the silence of the brightening dawn, before anybody found us.

He held the deck door open for me. I tiptoed past him to the kitchen. While I was tossing the unopened bag of cookies onto the counter, he grabbed a pear from the fruit bowl and bit in. Slurping, he held it out to me.

"No," I whispered. "Remember? Those pears sucked."

"On Monday. Monday pears are hard and unripe. But it's Thursday now. Bite."

I took a bite. He was right. It was perfect, juicy and full of pear flavor. I stretched to take another just as he pulled the pear away and took one himself. We cracked up silently, and then he held it out again to me—but yanked it away before I could bite and took it for himself. So I had to grab his wrist and hold the pear steady to get another one in. "Yum," I whispered. He took a last bite before holding it out toward my mouth. Despite the sticky mess, sharing that pear felt even more intimate than the kisses out on the deck.

By the time he tossed the core into the garbage disposal in the kitchen sink, the light coming through the window was dayish enough to see each other clearly. His hair was rumpled and his lips were puffy red, with a bit of pear juice just off the center. I'm sure I looked similarly worse (or better) for wear.

He wiped his sticky hands on his pajama pants and grabbed my hand. "Come on," he whispered.

Our hands stuck together as we dashed around the corner to the stairs. He stopped short on the landing. Our parents were behind a door just above us. I made a face like *Go! Go!*

He grinned back at me, leaned toward me.

I shook my head and pushed him up the steps.

At his room, he stopped again and turned around, grabbing me by the sleeve of my fleece and pulling me toward him. "This is fun," he whispered in my ear.

There was a noise from behind our parents' door. His eyes opened wide and mine did, too. I scurried down the hall. At my bedroom door, I turned around. His head was peeking out from behind his.

"See you at breakfast," he mouthed.

I rolled my eyes and dove into my bed. My mother's alarm clock buzzed before I was fully under my covers. I froze, listening, as some whispering and then some giggling wafted down the hall from her room toward my unwilling ears, until I had the sense to cover my head with my pillow.

In the silence and darkness, I didn't plot out how in holy hell I was going to get through breakfast and the day of school—Spirit Day, I remembered in my fog; have to wear a purple shirt. But I didn't jump up to make sure my purple shirt was clean, or contemplate what I had gotten myself into and how many ways it could end in complete catastrophe (and how few, well, how *zero* ways it could end well). Or whether I'd tell Tess what had just happened. Nope. I fell asleep thinking forward twenty hours or so, to when maybe we could meet out on the deck again.

fourteen

I BLAME THE lack of sleep. But when my mother announced at breakfast that she had changed her mind about my sleepover Saturday, I think I was slightly justified in losing it, even if I had been in a normal state of mind.

Though how could I possibly be in a normal state of mind in front of Kevin and his family at breakfast, while having a should-be-private conversation with my mother despite my kiss-swollen lips?

She changed her mind. Saturday wasn't going to work after all.

"But I already invited people," I protested. "Tess will be so—I can't just cancel!"

"People?" Joe asked. "How many people were you planning on?"

"Excuse me?" I said. "I wasn't talking to—"

"Charlie," Mom interrupted. "We just think—"

"We?" I may have been yelling by this point. Just what I did not need was to cancel on Tess.

"Charlie," Mom said in a *Calm down NOW* voice. "Joe and I discussed it—and . . ."

"And he said no?"

She opened her eyes wide at me like *Let's discuss this later, not in public,* but we were not in public; we were in our own kitchen. And she was letting this guy take over what I was allowed to do or not even after she gave permission.

"That's not fair, Mom," I said.

"Charlie, come on now."

"Why can I suddenly not have friends sleep over?"

"Well, for one thing, what about Kevin? It doesn't sound fair to . . ."

"He could invite some of his friends over, too," I suggested, trying to sound both spontaneous and reasonable. "I don't mind. That's fine."

"Never gonna happen," Joe said. "Coed sleepover? Ah, no."

"That's not what I meant," Mom said, her hand on Joe's arm. "My point was, I wasn't really thinking of this when I said yes, but now I realize it could be uncomfortable, for Kevin, to suddenly have five girls . . ."

"Five?" Joe asked.

"Doesn't sound uncomfortable to me," Kevin piped up.

"Sounds like my birthday and Christmas all wrapped up in—"

"Kevin!" Joe said, but I could see he was sucking his smile in, trying not to laugh. Every once in a while, I get a glimpse of Joe's fun side and it really throws me off.

"Hey, that's a good idea," Mom said.

We all turned to her, like, *what* is a good idea?

"Why don't you postpone, have the sleepover during spring break? Kevin and Sam will be out west, so you and your friends can have some space, and . . ."

"I'm going to Dad's," I objected.

Mom hesitated.

"I'm not going to Dad's?"

"He's taking his wife and ABC to Paris that week."

"I thought he hated France," I said, despite completely not wanting to discuss this in front of the Lazarus family.

Mom's lower jaw tightened twice. She raised her eyebrows while shaking her head and said, "I thought he did, too." A small, mirthless chuckle escaped her.

"He's not taking me with them?" I asked in an unfamiliarly small voice. Not that I would want to go on vacation with them, where I'd basically be an unpaid nanny, but still.

"Maybe call your father later to discuss it?" Mom suggested. "And also the job thing? But meanwhile, wouldn't that be a better idea, postponing your sleepover until then?"

I shook my head, not trusting my voice, not trusting anything.

"Sure! You girls can rent some movies, and I'll get one of those tubs of popcorn for you, and Joe and I will mostly stay upstairs, and it won't be so awkward for Kevin, and it will all be good."

"The end," Samantha said without lifting her head from the book she was reading. She said it like the narrator at the end of a sweet little tale for children. I had to laugh a tiny bit at that.

"We gotta run," Kevin said, and thrust my bag at me. "Bye!"

We were out the door before I could even continue arguing or figure out what had happened.

"I can't believe her," I grumbled on our dash to the bus, which was pulling toward the corner already. "Or my father. Damn. Screw everybody."

"Better this way," Kevin said. "We'll tell them they can go out for dinner Saturday, then get Sam to sleep early . . ."

I opened my mouth in disbelief and gave him a little shove.

"I was just thinking we'd watch a movie," he said. "You're the one with the dirty mind."

"So are you," I said, climbing up the bus steps.

"Yeah," he said. And for the first time, he didn't pass me to go sit in the back row with Brad. He plopped down next to me instead.

I didn't ask him anything about his mom or tell him anything about my father. We didn't talk at all, in fact. For once I didn't get all awkward and compulsive about filling in the silences. I closed my eyes and slumped beside him, this hot guy I still didn't know all that well who had just witnessed private, inside family stuff, stuff nobody had gotten to witness before. Maybe somebody with siblings would feel different, but for me, it's always been me on my own, with only my mom or my dad for *discussions*. It was kind of embarrassing—*whose father disses her like that*? But I'd witnessed some of his secrets, too, I realized. We might tilt our heads down toward our feet during moments of odd family tension, but still there was no way to avoid getting some inside views, simply by living in the same house as each other.

I felt his knee fall against mine as the bus went around a curve. I didn't open my eyes or move my leg away, and when the torque straightened out, his leg continued pressing warmly against mine. I opened my eyes, an adrenaline surge waking me up fully, better than anything Anya could whip up at Cuppa, for sure. I spent the rest of the ride looking out the window, silent, with my thigh and Kevin's pressed against each other, so anybody could see if they looked.

As we rounded the corner coming up to school, Kevin held out his hand to me. In his palm was cradled a pear, the last one, ripe, from the fruit bowl. I took it, held it against my chest, and let it slip into my bag before we got off the bus. I didn't say thank you out loud, but I could tell he heard it anyway.

I passed Tess a note in bio that my mother had lost her mind or at least changed it because of her husband, so my sleepover was canceled. She didn't write back, but she did wait for me, to walk through the hall together.

"Hey, sorry I didn't tell you I was trying for the job at Cuppa. I . . ."

She shrugged. "Think you'll get it?"

"Yeah, I did, actually."

"You get a discount?"

"Twenty percent off."

She looped her arm through mine. "That'll help."

My face unclenched. I may even have taken a note in class.

At lunch, all the girls gathered around me, commiserating as I told them about my mother's horrible new flirtiness and mind-changing, and how Kevin's father was almost always *there*, in my house, and how I can't even ever leave the bathroom door open anymore.

"Does Kevin walk around in a towel?" Felicity asked, leaning close, her hand on my arm.

"Yes," I whispered, and everybody shrieked.

"He is such a slut," Tess said. "I'm sorry, Charlie, I know you're stuck with him in your house, which has to be the most horrid, awkward thing, but I just have no use for him anymore."

"I'd find a use for him in a towel," Felicity whispered.

As she said the word *towel,* Kevin appeared in front of us like the ghost of Hamlet's father, and we all shrieked again.

At least he wasn't in a towel. His feet in their scuffed sneakers were spread wide apart, his jeans a bit frayed at the back edges. His dusky, gray-blue T-shirt was untucked, and over it he wore an unbuttoned, blue-and-white-striped button-down. His arms hung lankly by his sides, with his crumpled-top lunch bag gripped loosely in his left hand. When I finally let my eyes wander up to his face, I saw, as I expected by then, that peculiarly Kevin-ish look of patient curiosity, his head tilted slightly to the side and forward, his soft, red lips almost curving into a smile but not quite, his right-cheek dimple hinting at indenting. But his eyes were not vague or hinting. They were unwaveringly staring right into mine.

"Hi, Kevin," I said, striving for normalcy but apparently missing, because all around me, the girls other than Tess were giggling and collapsing onto one another, gasping for air, repeating, *Hi, Kevin! Hi, Kevin!*

Tess's eyes were pinched nearly closed, looking back and forth between me and Kevin.

"I got your lunch," Kevin said.

"You what?"

"Cheese sandwich?"

"Maybe it's your cheese sandwich," I mumbled.

"Nope."

I grabbed my lunch bag, or what I'd thought was mine, and opened it. There was a huge, round mound wrapped in tinfoil instead of my normal flat sandwich.

"Turkey and tomato?" Kevin asked.

"I don't know. It's huge."

"That's what she said," Darlene whispered behind me.

Kevin didn't glance over at her, or at anybody but me. "I

like it on a roll. You should try it."

Darlene and Paige were giggling behind their hands.

"Ignore them, Kevin," Felicity said, which shut them both up.

I stood up to trade bags.

He leaned toward me and let his fingers brush mine during the lunch bag exchange. "Did you eat the pear yet?"

"About to," I answered. "Thursday pear."

"Mmmm." He walked away, back toward the boys.

When I sat down, trying to look normal, Tess was glaring at me. "What the heck was that?"

"I must have grabbed the wrong—what?"

"Thursday pear?"

"It's a . . ." The words *family joke* strangled in my throat. "It's a pear. It's Thursday. What?"

"You guys sound like you're . . ."

"What?"

"Married," Tess said, at the exact moment that Felicity said, "Siblings."

We all opened our mouths wide at both ideas and how definite both Tess and Felicity had sounded. I tried to make it about Tess and Felicity, their conflicting ideas, but everybody was like, *Wow, Charlie, your face is so red*. I denied that, even though I could feel the heat fevering up my head.

We all just focused on our lunches for a while. I was concentrating too hard to say anything, working on not making eye contact with Tess, who would see the truth with her X-ray best-friend vision. At the same time, I was using every eye muscle I had on not lifting my gaze to Kevin's, to see if he had heard what Tess and Felicity had said and if he was still, over across the way where the boys were slouching, looking at me.

fifteen

AFTER SCHOOL I went straight to Cuppa. Anya had said
if I didn't have too much homework, I could stop by, maybe
learn how to clean the machines, maybe even make that pot
of tea she got too busy to teach me how to make the day
before. I wasn't scheduled to have an actual work day yet; I
had a bunch of training to do first, but she told me not to
worry, she'd pay me for training, too.

I didn't tell her I wasn't worried about that because I actually had no interest in the money at all. It would just sit in a
jar on my desk. There was nothing I wanted that money could
buy. I was just happy to have someplace to go instead of straight
home. On my way into Cuppa, my cell phone buzzed in my
pocket. My first thought was *Kevin* instead of *Tess*. Before I
could wonder what that meant, I saw that it was my mother.

Hi, Charlie!
I have a ?

My mother does not normally text me. She is a history professor at Harvard. Anything post–Civil War tends to strike her as disarmingly modern.

What's up? I texted back.

Does Kevin like it

Okay, I just stared at that for a few seconds. What the heck? Does Kevin LIKE IT?

I texted back:

????

I stood there and waited for a response. Finally, my phone shook again. My mom had texted:

Sorry. Does Kevin like IT

So I had to text back:

Mom what the heck is that supposed to mean?

Nothing. My phone just faked innocence, lying still as a walnut in my palm.

"You have to press something to make those work," said a voice beside me.

"Excuse me?" I looked way up into a scraggly but familiar face. It was a guy from school, a senior with heavy-lidded eyes and a hipster's slouch. Tall and slim, with dirty-blond hair hanging limp down his long neck. Rollerblades on his feet, a messenger bag slung across his torso.

"Oh," I said. "Hi." I had met him a few months earlier and seen him around, here and there. I groped my mind-files for his name, so I'd seem less little-girl frightened by his aggressive mellowness and sudden appearance. "Tony, right?" I asked.

"Close enough," he answered.

"Okay." Then my phone buzzed again. He looked over my shoulder at it.

Do you if Kevin likes

"My mother has lost her mind," I said.

"Who's Kevin?" Toby asked, raking his fingers back through his hair. "Your brother?"

"No, my . . . jeez. No! He's not my—never mind. My, he's my, my friend. Kind of."

"Boyfriend?"

"No!"

"Your mom is wondering who he likes?"

"No! What?"

"Who does she think Kevin likes?"

"I have no idea. I don't think she . . ."

"That's kind of cute, that your mom wants to know who your friend likes. Weird, but . . ."

"*Weird* doesn't begin to describe my family these days."

"Yeah, tell me." He skated forward and opened the door of Cuppa. I walked in. He followed me.

"Can I help you?" I asked him. The last thing I needed right then was a stalker, even one with a rumbly, slow-talking way and Rollerblades.

"No, I'm good," he said, and skated toward the counter, then around it, back to the storage room. Nobody stopped him; nobody who worked there seemed to be around, just me and this guy, gliding to the storage room to, whatever, steal all the coffee filters.

"Hey!" I yelled in my toughest voice, shoving my once-again-buzzing phone into my pocket. "Hey, you, not-Tony! You can't go back there! Hello?"

It was up to me, apparently, to stop him and save Cuppa from disaster. Awesome. I took a deep breath and charged across Cuppa, without a plan other than maybe to deck him.

I got bounced back to the counter when we slammed into each other. He was emerging from the storage room not with arms full of stolen merchandise but instead tying a Cuppa apron around his waist.

"You want a decaf, maybe?" he asked me. The skates were gone, replaced by TOMS. How was he so fast?

"No." I sucked on my knuckle, which had bumped against the counter.

"Oh, great!" Anya said, coming from the milk station near the bathroom. "You've met. Toby, this is Charlie, the new kid."

"I had a feeling," Toby said, nodding slowly, his eyes half-closed. "Cool."

"Can you give Charlie a manual and an orientation?"

Toby turned around and went to the back room. As Penelope emerged from under the counter and began her listless dance among the machines, which hissed and burbled under her care, Anya kept up a happy little chat with the elderly couple waiting for their drinks. I took up space.

Toby came back. He handed me a crisp Cuppa apron and a manual about seventy pages long.

"You gotta memorize that," he said. "Quizzes every single shift."

"You are frigging kidding me."

"Yes," he said. "Very few quizzes, for real."

I flipped through. There were pages and pages of precise measurements for every type of beverage; brew times; how many pumps of syrup flavoring go in which size cup; definitions—I was getting sleepy just skimming the headings. Expectations for what baristas and expeditors must do, say, and wear. "No tattoos," I read aloud.

"No visible tattoos," Toby corrected.

"Oh?" I looked. He was right. I tried not to wonder if he had any invisible tattoos.

He smiled. "Put it down for now. First rule of Cuppa is . . ."

"Don't talk about Cuppa?" I asked.

He smiled. "Yeah. Only other rule is, chill."

"Chill?"

"It's not pulling babies from a burning building, you know?"

"Yeah, but—"

"People are here to spend more on a cup of coffee than a Guatemalan guy makes picking coffee beans in a week."

"That's depressing."

He shook his head. "Everybody's day is what it is. May as well enjoy the one you're having, yeah?"

"Um, okay," I said.

"So you just give them some kindness with their cuppa. Even the ones who start their order with the dread word 'Gimmea.'"

"Gimmea?"

"Yeah. 'Gimmea tall, skinny latte?'"

"Oh," I said. "I hate that!"

"Right. Those people don't tip, either. Still."

"Be kind. Okay." I put the manual down on the one stool behind the counter. "So where do we start?"

Toby picked up the manual and handed it to me. "Senior person on the shift gets the stool. There's lots of rules. Most important one, though, is . . ."

"Chill," I said.

"And beware the evil frother."

"I will beware," I said.

Over the next hour I managed to mess up approximately

everything Toby attempted to teach me. When I pulled out the brewer, which I thought I was supposed to do, the grinds and hot water splashed out with tidal force and then stuck like molten tar to my hands, all the way up my wrists. I was talking, at the time, to a supernice and patient woman, who kept telling me not to worry.

Penelope, meanwhile, stood beside me, behind me, ultimately in front of me, fixing the stuff I messed up, which was, well, everything I laid my hands on. After I shredded yet another garbage bag with a long line of customers waiting, Penelope suggested I haul the garbage out back to the Dumpster and take my allotted ten-minute break.

"But Toby's not back from his," I started to object.

"It's okay. I got this. Go." It was not an offer made from generosity, clearly, but in a desperate effort to take a break from my incompetence. I didn't blame her, or mind.

"Thanks," I said.

"Take as long as you want," she added.

Every part of me was tired. I lugged the heavy bag over my shoulder like Santa's loser little sister and backed out the door to the alley. Into the Dumpster it went, and I nearly followed, but I didn't have the energy. I slumped against the wall instead.

"Having fun yet?" Toby asked from up the steps beside the Dumpster.

"Oh yeah," I said. "Tons."

"Didn't figure you for the working type."

"No?"

"Student council or something."

I sat down on the bottom step, a few lower than his feet. "Nah. Not a rah-rah girl."

"So much for first impressions. The money's not bad here."

I didn't respond. I had eight more minutes, and the possibility of dozing off was very real.

"You may be the least naturally gifted barista I've ever seen," he said.

"Call Guinness," I said.

"Or Ripley's," he added. "How's the burn?"

I closed my eyes. "Which one?"

He held out his hand in front of my face. With supreme effort, I opened my eyes halfway, to see. He had little scars all over the backs of his hands.

"All from here?" I asked.

"Most," he said. "Most people don't last past orientation."

"I'm as disoriented as I've ever been."

He chuckled.

"And that's saying a lot. But this is the only place in my world that hands out a manual of expectations and rules, so, gotta love that."

"Indeed. And at the end of the day, you go home with money you have truly earned. Pretty sweet, that." Toby stood up and held his hand out to me. "You coming back in, or no?"

"In six minutes," I answered as my eyes closed again.

"Cool," he said, stepping past me.

sixteen

WHEN I GOT home three hours later, Mom and Joe were cooking together, giving each other tastes with spoons and laughing. "Hi, Charlie!" Mom said as I passed.

"You guys are gross," I answered. It smelled good in there, but it was too hot and steamy, in every inconceivable way.

"How was work?" she called after me.

"Um," I said, yanking myself up the stairs with help from the banister.

Kevin's door was closed, I saw as I reached the top of the stairs.

The next thing I noticed was that all along the hall walls were photographs. Very arty, I admit. Maybe too arty. Self-consciously arty, black and white, lots of partial faces and shadows. And most of them were of Kevin, or Samantha, or Kevin and Samantha.

I was standing in the hall looking at an especially gorgeous shot of Kevin as a little guy, maybe seven, sitting on a rock with one eye closed and the other open, glaring at the camera, when Samantha emerged from her room.

I jumped and dropped my backpack, in my failed attempt to not look guilty and *caught*.

"Do you want to play with me?" Samantha asked. "Or I could just read or hang with Alpha if you're busy."

"Hang with your fish?"

"If you're busy. Kevin has a lot of work, so you probably do, too, unless you're much more focused. I think he spends a lot of time on the internet. Also, he had baseball tryouts today."

"Yeah."

"He made the first cut. That means he still has a chance. Luckily, or he'd be a grouch and end up in a fight with my dad."

I smiled at her. A girl who spills too much, in hopes of connecting: my kindred spirit.

"So anyway, Charlie, if you have time and you want to watch a movie or play something together, I'm allowed tonight. I saved up my screen time and finished my homework."

"Oh," I said. "Okay." She was going to hang out with her *fish*? "I'm kind of wiped out, but let me try to get my home-work done and then maybe we can do that."

She smiled hugely.

"Is your tooth loose?" I pointed at the bottom tooth that was tilting out of her mouth.

She nodded and wiggled it for me.

"Ew. Wow."

"I am deciding to still believe in the tooth fairy."

"Good idea. I'll . . ." I pointed to my books and hurried to my room and closed the door. On a sticky note I wrote *tooth fairy*.

By the time we got called down to dinner, I had finished most of my work, other than math and an essay on Act Two of *Hamlet*. All the way along my previously peaceful, bare-walled hallway, the sometimes solemn and occasionally delighted faces of Samantha and Kevin stared out from beautiful photographs.

"Did you finish?" Sam asked eagerly as I slipped into my seat.

"Almost. How's the tooth?"

"Wiggly."

The kitchen smelled amazing—warm, garlicky, but also like just-mowed grass in spring. Joe ladled a mass of green slime–covered spaghetti onto my plate.

"I was going to surprise Joe and make lasagna, or maybe some other kind of pasta," Mom said, smiling so huge her gums showed. "That's why I was texting you, Charlie, to ask if you knew whether . . . well, anyway. But then I got home and Joe was already working on a pasta dinner!"

"Wow," I said. "Small world."

Mom's smile faded, just a bit. Why am I so reflexively obnoxious to her sometimes? Just because she's happy? Giddy in love? Why would I be mean about that? Why hadn't she asked my opinion on putting up pictures in the hall? I looked down at the gooey, green pasta strands tangled in the bowl in front of me. I had my doubts but took a taste.

It was so delicious I had to close my eyes and just taste for a minute.

"So?" Joe asked.

"This is really good," I had to admit. "Wow. Yum."

"Pesto," Joe said. "My special recipe—with cilantro, but no cheese."

"It's amazing," Mom said.

"We're all lactose intolerant," Joe said cheerfully. "The three of us. Too much dairy and we're all gas machines."

"Dad!" Kevin yelled.

"TMI," I said.

"Sorry," Joe said. "Well, anyway. We always have Lactaid with us, but with this recipe, we don't even need it!"

"Dad, do everybody a favor," Kevin said. "Stop talking."

Joe shrugged bashfully, and when I gave him a pity smile, he winked at me. Seriously. Winked. Exactly the way Kevin winked at me once. My hands, in a sudden attack of boingi-ness, flayed around and knocked over my water glass.

Water flew up in an arc and then splashed down all over the table and across it onto Kevin's lap. Trying to grab my napkin, I karate-chopped my knife, which did a little acrobatic routine in the air and landed on my foot, but luckily didn't slice it off, just clanged against it. I bent down to get it and banged my head on the underside of the table, coming up.

In all it was forty-five seconds of the Charlie Freaks Out Show.

The other four people at the table sat still and watched it. I resumed my seat as the water that had been in my glass drip-drip-dripped off, onto the floor.

"The End," I said.

Samantha giggled.

"Towel?" my mother suggested.

I went to the oven, where the towel wasn't, anymore. "I put up a hook," Joe said, pointing to the corner near the sink, where indeed a fresh new towel was hanging.

After I mopped up the mess, and managed to eat the rest of the dinner without smashing anything else off the table or onto anyone, I said, "That was great, Joe; thanks," and cleared my plate.

My mother, clearing her plate beside me, whispered, "You okay, Charming?"

I started to say, *Yes, sure, of course*, but it didn't come out. I nodded instead, and Mom put her arm around me. I still had my plate in my hand, so I kind of stood there, stiff and awkward. I had a sudden need to cry. No idea why. Just tired, I guess.

Mom took my plate out of my hands and turned me toward her. She hugged me hard and we just stood there. I didn't say, *Why does there have to be a new hook?* Because, seriously, why would a sane person cry about a very nice hook holding a towel in a more convenient spot, just because that is not where the towel belongs? What is so sad about that?

Everything.

I think some Lazarus people started coming to the sink with their plates, but Mom must have gestured to them to go away. I kept my eyes closed.

After a few minutes, the feeling passed. I took a deep breath and pulled away, bracing myself for questions and A Talk. But Mom, luckily, hadn't changed that much. She kissed me on the forehead and let me go.

"Hey, Sam," I said. "I'm pretty much done with work. Wanna hang?"

I saw Mom smile at me, out of the corner of my eye.

"Yes," Samantha answered. "Do you like games of luck or of skill?"

"Not really, no," I said.

"Oh. It was, I meant that as a choice."

"Having not too much of either puts me at a disadvantage," I explained.

"I could play down a queen, if you want to play chess," she offered.

"Okay."

She smiled, revealing her chaotic teeth. "I used to be scared of losing, too."

"I'm not scared," I defended myself, absurdly, to her. "Well, not terrified. Not of losing. Not at chess, anyway."

"Just remember," Samantha said solemnly. "At the end, whether you win or lose, we shake hands and both say *good game*. Winning feels better, of course, but either way, you end up with a handshake and a *good game,* so really you have to focus on the fun of playing instead of the dread of losing."

She might have weighed sixty-five pounds. I towered like a giant over her. Maybe she was Yoda.

"Or I could be wrong," she hedged.

"No, I don't think you are," I said.

She grinned.

"We have a chess set we got for Christmas around here somewhere," I told her.

"I can get my tournament set, if you want."

"Sure."

She ran up to her room and got her chess set. "Good luck," Kevin whispered. "She's really good."

"How do you know I'm not?"

"I know you are," Kevin whispered. "But maybe not at chess."

"I rock," I said. He nodded, heading upstairs.

I waited in the living room, while Mom and Joe went downstairs to shoot pool and drink wine. I tried to block out the sounds of their flirtation and pool balls.

Samantha came back down wearing her Ugg slippers, the same as mine because my mother bought them for both of us, and with an oblong canvas case slung over her shoulder. "Black or white?" she asked, already on the floor with her legs in a broken W shape around her.

"I don't care," I said. I looked away from those Uggs on her feet. It made no sense at all for me to be jealous of them, or of my mother's attention to this sweet, odd kid. What did it rob from me if my mother wrapped her up in cuddles and braided her hair sometimes? Nothing. Nothing.

Sam smiled to herself, her face bent over the mat of a chessboard, which she had taken from the case, unrolled, and was populating with big, solid chess pieces.

"I should warn you, I am a champion chess player," I said, sitting in front of the black pieces opposite her. I consciously loosened my vise-tight jaw.

Paling, Samantha opened her huge eyes wider. "Really? You are?"

"No," I said, my tight meanness melting in the heat of her earnest tension. "I just thought I should tell you that. To throw you off. Even though it's a lie."

"Okay. White moves first," she said, and plopped a pawn into the middle.

Ten seconds later, before I'd found a comfortable way to sit, she said, "Mate."

"*Mate* like you're affecting an English accent? Or *mate* like you win?"

"See?" She pointed at my king.

"Rematch," I said, not seeing.

The fourth game I lost in five moves, a personal best, which emboldened me. Fifth game, I got a sixth move. Sam's face furrowed as she studied the board.

"I'm trying to figure out your strategy," she said after a minute.

"Should I tell you?"

"No." She studied the board some more.

My butt fell asleep. I got busy wondering what kinds of cookies might be hidden in the back of the cabinet, and whether I had anything funny I could post on Tess's wall.

Samantha said, "I can't figure it out."

"Ah. My plan is complex," I said with as much drama as possible. "Try to stay with me here."

She nodded, her eyes lasers on the board.

"I was thinking, *Hmm. I haven't moved the horsie in a while.* So I moved it."

"The knight?"

"Okay," I said.

"Really?"

"Sorry. Your stepsister is kind of an idiot."

She jolted upright, startled.

"What?" I asked.

"My whole entire life I wished for a sister," she whispered. "My entire life."

"Me too," I said, not knowing if that was true or not,

before that moment, when it irrevocably was.

She started to smile a bit, but pulled it down, turning her eyes to the board again. She moved, I moved, she moved and said, "Mate."

I held out my hand again. "Good game."

"Good game," she said, shaking on it. "You shouldn't say nasty things about people. Even yourself. That's what my mom says."

I watched her put the pieces away carefully into their little plastic bags. "She's right, your mom. She's smart."

"Kevin hates her."

"No, I'm sure he doesn't."

"He does," Samantha said solemnly. "Because she left."

I nodded.

Samantha zipped up the canvas bag. "I don't hate her," Sam said. "I wish Kevin didn't. Do you hate your dad?"

"I don't know. I was really mad at him for a while. I don't really remember, but supposedly I wouldn't even look at him. It's like the one thing he and my mom agree about—how mad I was. And it took me years before I could even say hello to his girlfriend, who's now his wife. I just flat-out hated her. Maybe I still do. But I guess I don't hate him. Usually. And probably Kevin doesn't really hate your mom."

"He does," Samantha said. "Your dad got a girlfriend while he was married to your mom?"

"Yeah," I said, surprised by the catch in my throat. I didn't care anymore about that. Not really. I didn't think I cared, anyway. "Is that what happened with your parents, too?"

"No," Samantha said. I waited, but that was it.

"Mmm," I said.

She bit her lower lip. "I don't know. They just stopped loving each other, I guess."

"Oh."

"It's my bedtime." She stood up and extended her hand to shake again. "Thank you for playing with me, Charlie."

I stood up, too. "Your dad didn't notice the time yet," I said. "I could make us ice-cream sundaes, and we could gossip or something."

She hesitated. She definitely hesitated before she said, "No, I have to go to bed now."

"Okay," I said.

"Charlie?"

"Mmm-hmm?"

"Do you ever see swirly colors at the sides of your eyes?"

"No," I said. "Why?"

"Just wondering. I might be a mathematician when I grow up, or else a rock star."

"You'd be great as either," I told her.

"Thanks."

I stood alone in my living room and watched her drift upstairs in her clunky Uggs. I listened to her footsteps across the creaky hall.

With nothing left to do, I went up a few minutes later and wrote my *Hamlet* essay while listening to music with my earbuds in. I must have drifted off to sleep, because a while later, I thought Laertes was knocking at my door, but no, it was Kevin, in the ghostly hallway light, leaning against my door frame.

seventeen

STANDING THERE, SO still and back-lit, he looked like one of the moody photographs hanging in the hall come to life, as if the image had clambered out of the frame and wandered to my room.

I sat up and took off my earbuds, pulled them out of my computer, and shut it. He hadn't budged.

"Couldn't sleep?" I whispered.

He shook his head.

"I have to . . . I have to go to the bathroom."

"I'll wait for you in my room?" he whispered. "I need to talk to you. Okay?"

"Okay," I answered, and lowered my head. I couldn't meet his intense eyes; it made me turn all melty inside. *We have to talk* is a terrible phrase.

When he left, I quickly dashed to the bathroom, to pee and brush my teeth and figure out what the heck was happening. *He can't break up with me,* I thought; *we're not officially . . . anything.* Though that hadn't stopped me from breaking up with George, so I really had no good counterargument.

Not that you can argue logically when somebody's dumping you. It just doesn't matter. Even if you're right, you're still dumped.

But what if he didn't want to dump me? He didn't actually say, *We have to talk*; he said, *I need to talk to you.* Maybe he needed to confide in me. Unburden his troubled soul or some such horrible, wonderful thing.

For a girl who likes things clear and definite, I sure was making a murky mess of everything. I didn't know if Tess was my best friend now, or mad at me again. And Felicity? Were we suddenly buddies? And was George absent the past few days, or just really good at avoiding me?

Of course, that was all just a way to avoid thinking about the boy who was waiting to TALK to me a few steps away in his boxers and T-shirt, in his room, in my house. . . .

And also avoiding the fact that he had awakened me from a dream in which I was kissing Toby in that back alley, on those brick steps during a break, before Laertes showed up to sword-fight him.

I shook my head at myself in the mirror. *Get a grip, girl!*

I spat out the toothpaste and washed my face with the already damp (ew) bar of Dove soap. Another new thing: In my own bathroom, before, the soap was always dry when I touched it. Only *my* shampoo was in the shower. And the face towels were never soggy.

I tiptoed to Kevin's room.

"Hello," I said.

"Hi." He stood up and closed the door behind me. The lock clicked. His arm, still extended, hovered inches from my side.

"Hi," I said redundantly, and then, with goofiness jolting my nerves like electricity, I added, in a fake-husky voice, "We have to stop meeting like this."

"Why?" he asked in the intimate, unsmiling whisper of his.

"I don't know," I whispered back, breathing in the brisk, clean scent of Dove soap on both our faces, so close to each other, getting closer by the millisecond. "But, don't we?"

As an answer, he kissed me. Hard and full on the mouth, not tentative this time at all. I surprised myself by meeting him there, just as forcefully. I was out of breath in about three seconds, pressed up against the closed, locked door of Kevin's room.

It felt like thirst. Like when you're roasting hot in the summer, and all you can think is *water*. You're gulping from the water bottle, it's so good; the best anything ever. Even after the first few seconds, when you're no longer dying of thirst, you still keep wanting more, more, downing it, drowning in it, so fast it almost hurts. That's what it was like, this time, kissing Kevin.

Want want want. The word stopped making sense. Was that even a word? Or just a sound? Want. Wonton soup. Wanton girl.

What do normal people think about while they're kissing?

And then, without warning, there was this tenderness falling on us, between us, light like afternoon snow flurries. The kissing got slower, more gentle. His hands on my back pressed softer against my T-shirt, and then tangled up into my hair.

When I opened my eyes, his eyes were open, too, and he was staring at me with *tender* and *want* all swirled up together in his eyes.

"Chuck," he said.

"Mmmm," I said.

"Was the shirt I wore today purple?"

"What?"

He reached over to his desk and picked up his crumpled, blue-gray T-shirt.

"Blue," I said. "Grayish blue."

"Damn," he said. "I thought that one was the purple. Spirit Day."

"And here I thought you just had no spirit."

"This is why my favorite color is plaid," he whispered. "I hate being color-blind."

He looked so disappointed, I plucked the shirt out of his hand and flung it over my head. "Plaid's a good color."

"Is this, so, are you okay? With . . . this? Because . . ."

"Shhh," I answered, his answer, because I really was, I was okay with it and wanted to stay in that moment as long as possible. I didn't want to talk about it. I just wanted to experience it. I watched his eyes close again as his slightly smiling mouth met mine. He turned out the light, and then I felt his hand soft on my back again in the dark.

Soon, I'm not sure quite how, we were lying down together in the dark, private, secret night on his bed. His pillow smelled warm, slightly sweaty, and very, just, *boy.* I was starting to shiver a tiny bit, though, whether from fear or cold or something else entirely, I am not sure. He pulled up his nubby blue blanket on top of us.

We smiled a little at each other between kisses, our eyes closing, our fingers tentatively touching each other's faces, necks, collarbones, shoulders . . .

"Don't fall asleep," Kevin whispered.

"Mmm," I agreed, and pressed myself closer to him.

A minute later, it felt like, a knock pounded at his door. I fell off Kevin's bed onto the floor behind it.

I was instantly more awake than I'd ever been before, there in Kevin's bedroom in the glinting gold light of morning.

Knock, knock, knock.

eighteen

THE DOORKNOB TURNED and jiggled. Hearing it, I flattened myself on the floor.

Locked.

I thanked every god that had ever been worshipped.

Kevin cursed under his breath.

"Kevin?" Joe said through the mercifully closed door. "It's seven fifteen. You better get a move on or you'll be late for school!"

"Yeah, Dad!" Kevin barked back, not looking at me but throwing his blanket on top of my flat, quivering self. "On it."

As Joe's footsteps clomped toward my room with its open door and its lack of me in it, I could feel my eyes trying to pop themselves out of my skull. I sat slowly, silently up, crumpling the blue blanket in my lap but ready to flop back down under it if Joe stormed back toward us after finding me missing and, like, kicked in Kevin's door or something.

My life used to be completely plain and unappreciatedly boring. A morning trauma before all this was running out of Crispix.

From behind the bed I looked up at Kevin, not caring how wild-eyed and muss-headed I looked. Like it or not, we were in this mess together. We needed a plan, and quick.

Joe was down the hall, knocking on my door. "Charlie?" he called at my empty room. "Hey, Charlie?"

Finally, Kevin turned to me. I expected a mirror of my bat-crazy scared face, but he was smiling instead, his eyes sleepy but his mouth amused.

"We're so busted," he whispered to me, and then bolted out of his bed toward his door, his father's footsteps coming at us fast.

"Hey," I started to object, but when his hand hit the door-knob, I flopped down flat on the floor instead.

After he slipped out into the hall, closing the door behind him and convincing his father he was starving and in need of emergency poached eggs on an English muffin, Kevin went to the bathroom. I could hear him in there. How grossly intimate.

I took a few seconds to gather myself and then tiptoed to the door. No sounds out in the hall. I kept listening. Nothing. I opened the door a crack.

Samantha was in the hall outside the bathroom, reading a

book, waiting. She looked up and smiled at me. "Hi, Charlie," she said.

"Oh," I answered. "Hi."

She watched me walk past her from her brother's room to my own. I closed the door behind me and wilted against it.

I had to wait for Kevin and then Samantha to get through with the bathroom before I could get in there. Breakfast was another fabulous episode of *Charlie Collins, This Is Your Very Odd Life*, full of not making eye contact and lumps of granola drowning in yogurt.

Joe poured me a big glass of juice, and said, "Pulp Lovers!"

He held out his fist for me to bump. "Yeah, Pulp Lovers." I couldn't leave him hanging, so I bumped it, then said, "Let's never call ourselves that again."

"I think Pulp Lovers is a pretty awesome name."

"Uh, no," I said. "Really not."

I ate my Cap'n Crunch (we were out of Crispix) quietly and hid behind the newspaper while Joe quizzed his kids on their homework, hoping his question to me wouldn't be: *And where the heck were you this morning, young lady?* And there was no way I could possibly drink that big glass of pulpy juice, so if I got rickets or whatever it is you get from not enough vitamin C, it was fully going to be on his conscience.

My mother drifted down to the kitchen clutching a coffee cup and wearing nothing but her robe and a dreamy smile. I brought my half-empty bowl and full glass to the counter and didn't vomit.

On my way out the door to the bus, Joe called after me, "Hey! Charlie?"

"Busted," Kevin whispered, passing me.

"Hey," I whispered at his back. "What did you tell—we need to get—"

"Charlie?" Joe said again, this time right beside me. "We need to talk."

Don't pee in your pants, Charlie, hold it together.

"I know we are all getting used to living together."

"Mngrblrgh."

"And maybe this is—I should probably talk this over with your mother."

"No!" I said, perhaps a bit loudly. "Whatever you have to say? Just say it."

"I want us all to be respectful of, well, newly close quarters. And I don't want to get overly . . . I don't want to, don't want you to feel that I am . . ."

"Oh, for goodness' sake, WHAT?"

"I just think we have to be mindful that we are now, de facto, a family, and . . ."

"I changed my mind. Can we not talk about this?" I begged.

"I think we need to," he answered solemnly.

The bus was going to reach the stop in about two minutes. If he didn't hurry and tell me what a slut I was and I should stay away from Kevin, I'd be late for school, and have to walk all the way there. That kind of pissed me off, which was a relief. Better than quaking. I've only ever been late once in my life, the day I first kissed Kevin, and it goes on your permanent record. So I said, "You know what, Joe? It's none of your business, actually."

"Actually," he repeated, maybe mocking, his face reddening in blotches exactly the way Kevin's does sometimes. "It really is my business, Charlie."

My lower jaw slid out in front of my upper teeth, and my right knee thrummed back and forth with the effort of not fighting back against this man who was sleeping with my mother, living in my house, and, to be fair, had basically just caught me waking up in his son's room.

"If you don't wash out your bowl," he said, "I am the one who has to do it."

"My—what?"

"Your cereal bowl," Joe said. "I'd appreciate if you'd rinse it out and put it in the dishwasher from now on."

"My cereal bowl."

"After breakfast."

"Okay," I said.

"We'll all have to get used to one another, but I think mutual respect is the right way to start."

"Sure," I said. "Definitely." I squinted into the sun, toward where Kevin was a speck, at the end of the block. "I don't want to miss the bus."

"Oh, right; go. Absolutely."

"Okay." I stepped backward, away from him, down the step.

"Charlie," he said, and smiled happily, relieved almost,

when I turned around. "Glad we had this talk."

"Me too," I said.

"Have a great day!" he was yelling as I sprinted away from him. I made it to the corner just as the bus did. Kevin was already on by the time I started up the steps. "Well, that was weird," I said, slipping into the seat beside him. "Busted for lack of dishwashing."

His low chuckle warmed me almost as much as his arm, pressed along the length of mine.

I smiled at Tess between first and second periods, wishing with part of my brain that I could tell her everything, because she would double over laughing at the disconnect between what I thought I was going to be yelled at about and then actually getting a Talk About Not Washing My Bowl—but knowing in another part of my brain that it was kind of okay, keeping it to myself, too.

I walked to third with Jen, and for one second considered telling her, but came to my senses pretty fast when I remembered that, for one, her parents were friends with Kevin's dad and, for two, she'd get stuck on the part where I woke up in Kevin's bed and not jump right into how funny it was to be yelled at for dishwashing issues instead.

For a minute I sank into the sadness of no longer having a friend I could share absolutely everything with—but then that funk got crowded out by the sentence:

I woke up in Kevin's bed.

I didn't pay one bit of attention in math. That crazy sentence echoed around in my head, blocking out every other equation: me + Kevin over Kevin's bed divided by everything equals . . .

nineteen

"WHERE IS EVERYBODY?"

"I'll be with you in a . . ." My mother trailed off when I kept lurking around.

"It's Friday night," I mumbled. Who works on a Friday night? What did we used to do on Friday nights? Did she always hunch over her books and laptop like that? What did I used to do? It was not that long ago. Two weeks ago, what did I do on Friday night? Watch TV? Click around the internet?

I wandered into the kitchen to help myself to something to eat. I was most of my way through a Luna bar, staring blankly into the refrigerator, when Mom said, "I thought we'd go out."

I turned around. She was leaning against the counter, watching me carefully.

"Just the two of us?"

"Yes," she said evenly. Judging? Accusing?

"Why?"

"Spend some time together? Just, talk?"

They knew. Damn. Divide and conquer.

"Where's, where are, what about the other people?"

"'The other people.' Oh, Charlie." She smiled. "Joe's taking Samantha to a movie. Kevin is at a friend's house, sleeping over. Jared, maybe?"

"Brad?"

"Okay. And I thought maybe you and I would have a night just to ourselves. How does that sound?"

"Okay," I said warily.

She suggested we both change, or we didn't have to, and we could go to the Mexican place or sushi if I wanted.

"Okay," I said again.

"Why do you look so suspicious?" Mom asked me.

"I do not!" I yelled somewhat abruptly, and then stormed upstairs, past Kevin's quiet, empty room, to change into slightly different clothes. We ended up going for Thai food, because Joe doesn't like Thai.

Over curry and rice and pastel-colored crackers that disintegrated explosively on my tongue, I got questioned about friends, school, my life, and my adjustment to living as a family with the Lazarus clan.

Yes, I admitted, it has its awkward moments, since Kevin and I are in many classes together and also the same social group, yes.

"Joe thought maybe Kevin went out with Tess for a while

at some point," my mother said.

When I finished choking on a piece of chicken, I said, "Mom."

"Too awkward?"

"Yeah."

"Can I ask about you?" she asked.

"Me? What about—why are you—me?"

"I don't want to pry," Mom said.

"Good," I said, mopping my damp, sweaty face with my least-absorbent-ever-made pink napkin.

"I just want to, you know, stay up on what you're doing. Stay connected. It's important, with you in high school, and all these changes. The psychologist Joe and I spoke with recommended I should try to stay connected with you not just in terms of school but, regarding friends, too, and, romantically . . ."

Though I had vowed never to touch alcohol again, since I made my horrible Kevin-kissing confession after three shots of cheap gin at Darlene's party over the winter, I would have given a kidney right then for a gulp of my mother's Thai beer.

"Mom, no way. You spoke to a psychologist about me?"

"Not just you, of course," she said. "The whole situation."

I put my fork down on the table instead of through my eye. But it was close.

Mom wiped her mouth delicately with her napkin, laid it down in her lap, and leaned forward. Her hand covered the top of mine lightly, and her eyes squinted in that crinkly-kind/

smart way of hers. "Charlie. Let's be honest with each other."

"Why?"

She leaned back and laughed at that.

"What?" I was having a complete internal freak-out and she was *laughing*?

"Oh, I do love you, Charlotte Reese Collins. Why indeed?"

I tried smiling a bit. Failed.

She took a long sip of her beer. "That psychologist was so self-serious."

"Yeah?"

"Ugh. Yes! She was very convincing, too."

"Why did you, what made, why? A psychologist? Am I crazy?"

"No." She chuckled, as if I'd been kidding. "Charlie, no. Joe has found her a great resource in helping Kevin and Samantha, over the years since their mom left, and he has naturally discussed this new transition with her, with Dr. Jackson, I mean. So I went with him and we discussed the challenges that all three of you, all five of us, really, will be facing, and—"

"You *talked* about *me*?" The betrayal stung like a slap. "In front of Joe, with a stranger? You said stuff about me? Like what? Private stuff?"

"Yeah," Mom said. "I told her how you get constipated if you don't eat enough dried apricots."

"Still working?" the waitress asked.

"What?" I asked my mother, not the waitress, who backed

quickly away. "You didn't!"

"Kidding," Mom said. "Come on, Charlie. A little credit? We talked in general terms about our new situation and how it is likely to affect each member of our family."

"Our family," I echoed.

"Yes," she said. "Like it or not, we're kind of a family now. Aren't we?"

Instead of answering, I gulped my icy water and got an immediate ice-cream headache as a lovely parting gift.

"Well, we are," Mom said. "And Dr. Jackson thought, well, mentioned, actually had me almost convinced that it was going to be extremely awkward for you, as a teenage girl, with your emerging sexuality, and—"

"Ew! She said my 'emerging sexuality'?"

"Well . . ."

"And Joe heard?"

"Sure, he . . ."

"I am going to have to move, alone, to Alaska," I said, slumping against the bench.

"She said it was vital for me to stay connected to you, stay in tune with your feelings."

"My feelings."

"Yes."

"I'm feeling nauseated," I said.

"Me too," Mom said. "So I guess that's connected."

"We never really talked about that stuff before," I mumbled. "Who Tess is hooking up with, or whatever. Why would we have to start now?"

"Still working?" a different waitress asked.

"We never were," I said. "We were just eating."

Mom rolled her eyes at me but smiled. "We're all set," she said. "Just the check, please." After our plates were cleared, Mom leaned forward. "Maybe we'll get some ice cream on the way home."

"Okay," I said.

"Tess is hooking up with people?"

"Mom!"

"What does that mean, exactly, hooking up?"

The waitress put the check down in its vinyl folder between us. A tiny smile crossed her delicate face as she glanced at me. Laughing at me or feeling sorry for me? Did her mother ask her about her friends and their hook-ups?

I covered my face with my hands. "Fooling around," I whispered. "Making out. You know."

"Okay." Mom chugged the last dregs of her beer. "Fine. Good. Just checking."

After she signed the slip, we walked out through the cool night breeze toward the car.

"Are you?" Mom asked, pressing the remote to make the car beep and the doors unlock.

"Am I—what? Jeez, Mom. Seriously?"

"Not—I don't think you're having sex, but . . ."

"Ew!" I said. "Mom!" I was barely filling my B-cup bra. I got my period, what, a year and a half ago? And my first kiss six months ago? Outside school, that warm fall day with . . .

Do not think about kissing Kevin in front of your mother, Charlie!

"Mom, no. So far from . . . stop, please, and never go back to that horrible person who put these ideas in your head. We are not on some cheesy reality show. No!"

I pushed the image of waking up next to Kevin out of my mind as best I could, even squished my eyes tightly closed, but it stayed there anyway, the smell of his neck in my nose, the sound of his long hum-sigh, from somewhere deep in his throat and so quiet I could only hear the edge of it—it thrummed in my ears so loud it seemed completely possible my mother, beside me there on the dark, suburban sidewalk, could hear it reverberating from inside my memory.

I dashed away from her, toward the passenger side. With Joe missing, at the movies with Sam, I got my front seat back. It was probably too warm for the toast-your-buns feature, but I flipped the seat warmer on anyway while my mother fiddled with the ignition key. I waited impatiently for the engine to turn over so I could turn on the radio and AC to drown out whatever Kevin sounds and smells I was emitting.

"Hooking up," Mom said, looking straight into the rear-view mirror.

"What?"

"I was just wondering if you are 'hooking up' with . . ."

"Mom!"

". . . anybody. Because I have a feeling I know that you are."

Oh, crap.

"And who it is."

Aha. The actual reason for the fifty-dollar dinner and the divide-and-conquer strategy.

"So," she said. "Are you?"

"I'm just sitting here minding my own business," I answered.

Mom smiled dubiously. "You should take up dodgeball." She shifted into reverse. "Or fencing."

"Do I still get ice cream?"

"Is it George?"

"Is what George?"

"That you—you seem, kind of, distracted lately. And I was thinking maybe it's awkward for you to be—hooking up with a friend of Kevin's, and maybe Kevin is hooking up with your best friend, and—"

"Mom?"

"What?"

"You have to never say *hooking up*, ever again."

"Okay."

We rode along in silence. I turned off the radio, closed my eyes, and concentrated on the heat rising up from my seat.

"Is everything okay with you and Tess?" Mom turned to me at the light.

I didn't answer.

"She hasn't been over in forever, and . . ."

"And?" My eyes stayed closed.

"She didn't even come to the wedding."

I turned to Mom. She looked stressed, sad, both older and younger than usual—the parentheses around her mouth deeper, but the vulnerability in her eyes more pronounced, too.

"I'm sorry," I said, and started crying. Just a little.

A tear dripped out of Mom's eye, too. We both sniffed, at the same moment, as our hands, mirror images, wiped up at our noses the way my father hates.

"I'm sorry," Mom said. "I'm sorry, too. I don't want to be selfish, self-involved. I have so much going on, it's true—but if something is going on with you, I want . . ."

"Everything's fine," I said. "We went through a rough patch, me and Tess. We're better. Everything is fine."

"You're fine."

"I am," I said. "I'm fine. I'm good." I smiled at her, surprised because I meant it.

"Good," she said.

"And I'm happy you're happy, Mom. I know I don't always act like it, but I really am happy for you. Deep down. You deserve it."

She smiled really big at that. "Thank you, Charlie."

We ordered double scoops to go at Mad Alice's. As we neared the door, heading out with the ice cream in a bag, George appeared on the other side. "Hey!" I said, forgetting to feel awkward around him, because he looked momentarily so happy to see me.

"Hi, George!" my mom said, and went to give him a hug.

"Hi, Elizabeth," George said, hugging her back politely. "This is Sadie Wyatt. Elizabeth Reese. Charlie's mom. You know Charlie, right?"

"Hi, Sadie," I said.

"Hi, Charlie," Sadie, the smartest girl in tenth grade, said. "Nice to meet you, Elizabeth." Her light-blond hair was back in a loose bun, and her glasses, greenish rims that came almost to points at the edges, looked particularly cool and alternative. Sadie Wyatt and George? Really?

"Oh," Mom said, looking from Sadie to George to me again. "Um, yes. You too."

"We gotta go," I said. "Mom?"

"Yes," Mom said. "Bye."

"See you," Sadie said to me, and then, to my mom, "Nice to meet you, Mrs. Reese."

"Bye," George said.

Mom kept checking over her shoulder as they went into Mad Alice's together. "What . . . ," she said once we were safely behind closed car doors. "Why was George . . ."

"I'm not going out with him," I said. "I told you."

"You did? Is that—are you okay?"

"Yes. Can we just . . ."

She started up the car and I turned on the music, loud. When we got home, I went straight to the kitchen for spoons, and met Mom out on the deck, where we ate our ice cream in slightly awkward but companionable silence.

When Joe came home, he put Samantha to bed upstairs and stayed up there. Kevin was going to be out at Brad's all night. I leaned back against the deck chair and could almost imagine life was normal for a few minutes, until Joe appeared on the deck.

Mom gave him a taste of her ice cream with her spoon, and he hum-sighed as it melted on his tongue.

I said good night and headed upstairs to bed, lonely but blissfully unaware of what my friends were doing across town.

twenty

"HEY," KEVIN SAID, walking in through the back door with his backpack slung over one shoulder. He smiled all big and happy, like seeing me halfway down the basement stairs with a loaded laundry basket in my arms was a surprise birthday party for him.

"Hi," I said, grinning right back.

He kicked off his sneakers and picked them up by the backs. When he stood up again, his head was still bent toward the floor, but his eyes found mine. "Long time no see," he said.

Who even says that? Tess and I hate when people use clichés non-ironically. So I chuckled a tiny bit and said, "Yeah, right. Did you miss me?"

He nodded. "Turns out I did."

I leaned against the basement stairs' banister to keep from tumbling backward all the way down to my dirty-laundry-covered death.

"Did you miss *me*?"

"Weirdly enough . . . ," I answered, my voice shakier than I'd wanted it to be.

He took a step down and, in his hoarse whisper, asked, "Anybody else home?"

"Upstairs," I whispered back.

"Maybe we should go . . . check on something in the basement . . ."

"I'm supposed to put in this load of laundry."

"That'll do." He dropped his backpack and sneakers in the hallway. "I'll help."

His hands were on my waist before we got all the way down to the basement, and before we got to the laundry area, he had taken the basket from me. He set it on the floor beside the door that led to the laundry room. My back was pressed up against the wall with Kevin pressed up against me, when his father bellowed his name.

Kevin pulled his face away from mine and answered, "Yeah?"

"What do you think you're doing?" Joe called from one floor up.

I tried to wiggle away from Kevin, but he touched my hair lightly and smiled. "I have no freaking idea," he answered his father, looking right into my eyes.

"We've talked about this, Kevin, and I meant what I said."

"You *talked about this*?" I whispered frantically to Kevin, who shrugged and shook his head.

"Sorry!" Kevin yelled back with another shrug, and whispered to me, "No idea what he's talking about."

"One more time and I mean it, I am tossing your shoes out on the lawn again."

"Oh," Kevin said. "Right. Okay."

"Are you playing pool?" I saw Joe's shoe appear on the first step.

"No," Kevin answered. "Helping Charlie with the, uh, laundry."

"Oh," Joe said with a bit of disappointment in his voice. "Good. We can play pool later. Good idea to get our chores all done first. Good. Hi, Charlie."

"Hi, Joe," I called back, sounding suspiciously weird.

"You guys need help?"

"No!" both Kevin and I shouted, so I added, "We got it, thanks."

"Okay," Joe said. "Well, then, guess I'll see what I can do with these garbage cans."

"Sounds great," I said, and when Joe's foot retreated up the stairway, Kevin's mouth came down hard on mine again.

"Hey!" Joe called, ripping us apart again.

"What?" Kevin asked.

"Don't forget the fabric softener."

"On it," I answered.

We managed eventually to leave that spot in the basement and go to the laundry room, where we switched the dry clothes to a pile on the ironing board, the wet white clothes into the dryer, and the dirty clothes into the washer. When everything was thrumming in there, and we'd made out a bit more, I said, "We should go up."

"Why?" Kevin asked.

"Well, for one, we can't hear anything in here, like anybody coming . . ."

"I don't care," he said.

We kissed for another minute or two, and then I pushed him away. "You really did miss me," I said.

"Brad's not as fun at three a.m. as you are."

"No?"

He grinned and took the basket from me. "He has his moments, it's true," he said.

I pushed him up the stairs, asking, "Oh yeah? Does he?"

We sat down together in the living room, on the floor, to fold the dry laundry. It was deeply awkward. His boxer shorts, and his father's boxer shorts, were tangled up in my T-shirts and panties. We developed a system: Any time one of us got something that belonged to the other, or the other's parent, we just flung it at each other.

"You have hearts on your underwear butts," Kevin remarked.

"Shut up."

"Just saying."

"You have rocket ships on yours," I snapped back.

"Those are cool," he said.

"In third grade, maybe."

"And again in ninth," he insisted.

"Okay. And, in answer to boxers or briefs, you'd say both?"

"Depends on the occasion," he answered matter-of-factly. "Like, you don't want to be hanging loose if you—"

"Stop," I said. "I do NOT need to know this information."

"What information?" Mom said, peering into the living room. "Oh, thanks for folding, you guys. Do you have a lot of homework?"

"Yes," I said, as Kevin said, "Nope."

"Ah," Mom answered. "Because it's really nice out, and I was wondering if you guys would be willing to get the canoe out of the shed and bring it down to the beach. I thought maybe we could show these guys around the lake."

"Now?" I started to object.

"We're on it," Kevin answered, as if he were a kid on a sitcom in the 1950s.

Mom took a step back and said, "Well, then. Thanks, Kevin." She eyed me a bit suspiciously, so I shrugged.

"Charlie and I were just talking," Kevin said. "And—you and my dad haven't had much time alone, just the two of you. So if you guys want to go out to dinner tonight, Charlie and I could watch Samantha."

"Well," Mom said, smiling at him, her hands on her hips. "We were thinking we'd do a family night, maybe a movie or something."

"Just an offer," he said.

"Thank you," Mom answered. "I'll talk about it with your dad. You guys cooked this surprise up together?"

"We're just awesome that way," I said.

"You are indeed." She stepped into the living room, between us, and picked up her pile of clean clothes. "Lots of laundry, huh?"

"Lots of people," I said.

"Many hands make light work," said my mother, quoting her mother.

"Too many cooks," I said back, quoting the opposition.

Mom, who only uses clichés ironically, too, winked and left.

Kevin said, "Sometimes I have no idea what you two are talking about."

"We lived alone together a long time," I explained.

"Where's the shed?" he asked. "I like the sound of it."

Half an hour later, while we were making out amid the cobwebs and unused sports equipment in the shed, Kevin asked if I was buzzing or he was.

We stepped apart and checked our pockets. It was my cell, with a text from Tess, asking if Kevin was *there*.

"Why wouldn't she just text you if she wants to know where you are?" I asked Kevin.

"Dunno," he said. "Looks like my phone is dead."

"You can charge it."

"It's nice when it's dead. It's a break. I like it. You should try it sometime. Just disconnect completely."

"You want to go inside and call her from the house phone?"

"No."

"Well, what am I supposed to tell her?"

"Tell her, Kevin is here in my shed, trying to get under my shirt."

"Kevin!" I pushed him lightly. He bumped into a pile of life jackets, which toppled.

"Just don't answer," he suggested. "Forget her. She scares me."

"Scares you?"

"She's scary."

"She is not," I said. Pushing his hands off my waist, I texted back, *yes. Y?* and then suggested to Kevin that we try to get the canoe down from its perch on the top shelf, where it had wintered under a tarp.

Before we began, my phone buzzed again.

I have to talk w/u about him!

"Why does she have to talk with me about you?" I asked Kevin.

"I don't know."

"Does she know?"

"Know what?"

"About—us."

"Not from me," he said.

"So how does she know?"

"Why are you jumping to the—know *what* about us?"

"Kevin . . ." Was he denying that anything was going on? Or that he had told anybody? Did he just want to make me put it out there, between us, that obviously *something* was going on, something secret and big and . . .

"What?" His lake-blue eyes blazed darkly.

"What is Tess talking about?"

"I don't know," he said. "She's crazy."

"She's my best friend," I said. "And she has, like, a second sense of things. I think maybe she knows we're—we're, you know . . . whatever it is we are. Oh my god . . ."

"So ask her what the hell she's talking about, if you want to know."

He climbed up the shelves of the shed and shoved the canoe off the top. The pointy end of it came at me fast. I dropped my cell to catch the canoe as it speared through the musky shed air toward me, then stood there barely managing it while Kevin jumped from near the ceiling down next to me.

He grabbed the middle of the canoe and yanked, so it fell the rest of the way down toward us. The dusty tarp covered our heads. He had the bulk of the canoe's weight by then, so I could struggle out from under the tarp and then flip it off his head, too. Together we set the canoe down on top of the tarp, on the floor of the shed, and got our toes—but not my phone—out from under it.

"How much does that sucker weigh?" he asked.

"A lot," I said. "More than it seems."

"Surprised it doesn't sink."

"We'll see," I said. "Kevin, please just tell me what I should say to Tess, about us."

"I don't—Listen. I'm not interested in getting caught up in Tess's drama. It's all gossip with her, all Drama all the time, and it's stupid," Kevin whispered. "I don't want to go there. Been there, done that, and it sucked for both of us. Right?"

"Right," I said. His hands were gripping my waist again.

"It's so middle school."

"True," I admitted.

"I'm not like that. I don't . . ." He touched my chin gently with his long fingers. "No craziness. Huh? We're so separate from that. You and me. We're different."

"Yeah," I said, somewhere between agreeing and asking.

"You want to be with me, be with me," he whispered, and kissed my lips lightly. "You don't, don't. I don't care what people say or think, and neither should you. None of anybody's business. No bull. Just us, in that cool space where nobody else exists. Okay?"

"Okay," I said.

twenty-one

WE WERE ACROSS the lake in the canoe, me up front, Sam in the middle, and Kevin in the stern, when the sky darkened.

"I'm cold," Samantha said. "Is it supposed to rain?"

I turned around. Kevin was biting his lower lip, the paddle resting across his lap. Samantha was hugging herself on the middle seat.

"Maybe we'll head back," I suggested. The wind was picking up, and the current was pushing us toward the clubhouse, exactly across the lake from home, where we needed to head.

"Hurry," Samantha said. Her teeth were starting to chatter. "Why is it getting dark so fast?"

"Chill," Kevin said. "Everything's gonna be okay. Tell us what you're learning about in science these days."

"Gotta be better than our science class," I said.

"Migration," Sam said. "Is a storm coming?"

"Oh, I remember migration," I said. "When Ms. Channing first asked us if anybody knew the meaning of *migrate*, somebody said, 'Yeah, it's a really bad headache.' Some boy."

"Me," Kevin said.

"That was you?" I asked, rowing harder. Sam was right; it did look like a storm was rolling in, and fast. "That was hilarious. Didn't we all think that was so funny?"

"Maybe you did," Kevin said, pretend-abashed. I turned around. He winked at me. "I was being serious. Migraine, migrate. I was nine!"

"See those three birds?" Sam asked, pointing. "They're flying low. Birds fly low when it's about to rain."

"Three little birds." I smiled as reassuringly as possible at her. "You like reggae?"

"Bob Marley is the bomb," Kevin said. "We love reggae, right, mon? Sam?"

Samantha nodded. The silence hung thick around us. Nobody else was out on the lake. We'd worn fleeces under our life jackets, but it really had been pretty warm, warm enough to work up a little sweat on the way across. But now the temperature was dropping, and we were wasting time, me and Kevin, staring into each other's eyes, smiling at each other. It was nuts. I just felt so loopily happy, smiling at him in the gathering gloom, like a six-year-old at her own birthday party as the cake is coming out, brightening all her best friends' faces in the warm candle glow.

A drop of rain plunked down onto my nose.

"It's raining," Sam said. "It's raining and we're in a metal canoe on the lake. This is not safe."

"We're fine," Kevin told her, picking up his oar. "Call the route, Captain."

Kevin was the one who was supposed to steer; he knew how, he'd assured me, from summers at camp—and it was true, I could tell as we rowed out—but it was my lake, his first time on it. I had to choose our route.

Tess would have chosen, from Kevin's seat. I started to shrug, but I liked it that he wanted me to choose, trusted me to. Called me *captain*. Kidding, but not entirely.

So I stopped the shrug and thought. Across the lake was the straighter, shorter path; along the shore was longer but maybe easier than fighting the wind and the current. Or maybe not. "Straight across," I said, sounding more certain than I felt.

"Aye-aye, Captain," he answered. "Straight across it is."

I pivoted in my seat and started rowing. We lurched forward with pretty good power and speed. I kept my eyes on the speck of beach that was our property, and calculated we'd be there within ten minutes.

That's when the deluge started for real.

The drip, drip of the tentative first drops gave way to a ferocious dousing. The silence was roared away by the percussive rain, and by Samantha's screams.

Kevin and I just kept rowing, though we were barely making any headway. I turned to gauge how far we were from the clubhouse and consider maybe turning back, waiting out the storm there.

"What are we gonna do?" Sam shrieked.

"We're gonna row like hell for home!" I yelled back.

"We're gonna DIE!" Sam howled.

"Someday," Kevin told her. "Not today. Today we're just gonna get wet." He shook the water from his hair like a dog.

I rowed as hard as I could. When my shoulder burned beyond bearing, I switched sides. Behind me, I heard Kevin say something, so I yelled, "What?"

"Nothing!" he yelled back. "Singing."

Through the thumping rain and my thrashing paddling, I made out the tune. Bob Marley's "Three Little Birds." I joined in: "Every little thing's gonna be all right. Don't worry about a thing . . ."

We were slightly closer to shore when we finished the song. Sam had stopped screaming. Kevin and I kept rowing, the rain kept raining, though a bit less insistently now. Behind me, I heard Samantha start singing. It took me a few strokes to figure out what the song was: "You Are My Sunshine."

Kevin and I joined in with her, tugging at the lake, fighting for each inch: ". . . You make (pull) me hap (pull) py! (two strokes) when skies are . . . (row, row) You'll (closer, closer) never know (pull) . . . how much I (row) . . ."

"Love you."

The rain eased up. Not completely, but enough to make those words, LOVE YOU, sound like we were shouting them.

All three of us started laughing. I had to catch my breath for a second. I turned around. Kevin, rain dripping off his hair onto his face, winked at me.

I wiped my hair off my face and smiled at him.

"You guys!" Sam said. "We're not there yet."

I went back to rowing. We got through that song and then "This Little Light of Mine" and eventually "Row, Row, Row Your Boat," which we all agreed was way too annoying, so, with our patch of beach in sight, and on it our parents in bright-yellow rain gear, we sang at the top of our voices "The Star-Spangled Banner."

Our parents helped us pull the canoe in as they praised our patriotism and asked if we were okay. "We almost died," Samantha said calmly. "But instead we just got wet and sang."

"Good choice," Joe said, wrapping her shivering body in a towel. Mom handed me and Kevin each towels. She started to rub my arms to warm me up, but I stepped away.

"We were worried," Mom said.

"We weren't," I said. My arms felt as wobbly as Sour Power Straws, and I was that nauseating combination of hot on the inside and cold on the outside—but I don't know if I ever felt better.

Joe and Mom, with Samantha between them, started up toward the house.

Kevin was rubbing his hair with the towel, so he didn't see

them step away. I hung back. When he emerged from inside the towel, he draped it around his shoulders and reached out to touch my damp back, right between my shoulder blades.

"What's that amazing smell?" he asked.

I breathed it in. "Honeysuckle, I think."

"Mmmm." He pulled me closer. "Awesome rowing, Captain."

I leaned into him, just for a second, as we followed the others up the hill, and whispered, "Right back at you."

twenty-two

SAMANTHA'S EYELIDS WERE droopy, so Joe carried her up to bed. Mom sat in the living room chatting with me and Kevin. Kevin complimented her on the mac and cheese she'd made us while we were changing into dry clothes.

"From the box," Mom admitted.

"Where are you guys going to dinner?" he asked.

"Maybe we ought to skip it," Mom said.

"No," both Kevin and I said.

She looked a little surprised. "You should go," I added. "We'll hold down the fort."

"You sure?" she asked.

Joe came down holding his shoes. "Out like a light," he announced. "Should we go?"

"You feel okay about it?"

"Great about it." He wrapped his arms around her.

"We'll be fine," Kevin said.

"Let's go," Joe said, his hand on my mother's shoulder. "Back by midnight. Be good."

"I'm always good," Kevin said.

Joe sucked in his lips. I was getting used to his expressions, especially because Kevin had the same ones.

After the car pulled away, taillights blurring in the rain, Kevin and I stood somewhat awkwardly across the kitchen from each other.

"So," I eventually said.

"So." He leaned back against the counter. His hair was a little wavier than usual, with one whorl hanging onto his forehead. I had an almost irresistible urge to touch it. "Wanna watch TV?" I asked, stepping close to him, but keeping my hands to myself.

"Uh-huh, soon." He reached out and touched my hair. "That was fun, the canoe."

"Yeah." I wasn't smiling just about the canoe adventure but also the fact that he had a hair-touching urge at the same moment I did.

"What?" he asked.

"I like . . ."

"Me," he finished.

Well, yeah. And your hand in my hair. And how you smell, and how I feel shot through with electric current when I'm so near you, and how intimate it feels sharing secrets with you,

161

and . . . "I like how you are with Samantha."

"Me too," he whispered. "I mean, I like how I am with her, but also, how you are with her. Cool, but sweet. Strong. And sure. Fun."

I touched his arms with my hands. "You too."

"Mmmm. Plus I have an excellent singing voice."

"Well," I negotiated. "It is loud."

"Hey! But you have to admit I'm a champion rower."

"In your dreams. Though I did like how you followed my orders."

"You like that, huh?" He pulled me closer.

"I do."

"We're good, together. You and me. A good team."

"You think?" I asked, almost silently, so close to his face I had to close my eyes to keep from seeing double.

Not often, Tess would've answered.

"No. I know," Kevin whispered instead, and kissed my lips lightly. "We are."

"I guess we are," I agreed, kissing him back. "Good thing, because there's no escaping each other."

Our smiles dissolved. *No escaping each other* hung there in the air between us, as invisible and undeniable as cigarette smoke.

"Race you there," Kevin whispered.

"What?" I asked his back. "Where?"

I chased after him to the living room. He beat me by a step, and only because he boxed me out.

"Cheater." I grabbed the clickers while he flopped onto the couch. The sound came on blastingly loud. I lowered it and then sat down on the couch, in the corner, and clicked around looking for something decent to watch.

"This is good," he said, so I left it. The Red Sox were playing, down by two to the Yankees in the seventh. Our feet touched each other on the bench in front of us, and by the first commercial, my head was on his shoulder.

"This is really good," he whispered, lowering his mouth to mine.

By the bottom of the next inning, with men on first and third, we were both yelling at the TV.

During the commercials, Kevin muted the sound. I really like that in a person, but I didn't say so. It would have come out weird, I thought.

He returned my smile and asked if I could keep a secret. I swore I could.

"My dad's putting up a hammock tomorrow morning. He got it for your mom, a really nice one, as a wedding present. He's waking me up at dawn to help him. So I'm thinking, maybe you should stay in your own room tonight. Just saying."

I shoved him off the couch for that.

The game came back on and the score was tied, top of the ninth, so we had to focus. The dreaded Yankees scored, so we were both cursing, throwing hexes I'd learned from my grandmother at them. When the Sox came back with a game-winning, bases-loaded double, we jumped around like a couple of lunatics. Kevin swore his true love to my grandmother and hexes and lefty clutch-hitters. We toasted them and each other with our water bottles and switched the channel to wait for *SNL*.

"She hates hammocks, by the way," I said. "My mom."

"Not this one. This one's sweet."

"All hammocks. She gets seasick on them."

"Maybe you'll be surprised," Kevin said. "I think it was Gandhi who said, 'The time to make up your mind about people is never.'"

"Really? Gandhi?"

"What?"

"I like that, and it sounds familiar, but are you sure that was Gandhi?"

"Yes," he said. "I know stuff, too, you know. You're not the only . . . ugh, never mind."

"The only what?" I asked.

"Nothing. I don't know why you're mad at *me* all of a sudden."

"I'm not," I said. "I'm not. Sorry. I'm just, I can't find my phone, and I haven't talked to Tess since this afternoon, when she was in the middle of—damn, it must be in the shed."

"You don't need it. Shhh."

"No, you don't know Tess. She gets mad, and . . ."

Kevin shrugged. "She'll get over it."

"Yeah. No. Not really."

"You are not going out to the shed right now. Mice, bats . . ."

"Ew, no. Really?"

"Absolutely. I'm not going out there tonight. Stay here with me."

He kissed me lightly on the mouth. "Okay." I kissed him back. "Maybe you're right, and Gandhi's right. Or whoever."

"Mark my words. She'll love this hammock. Bet you a kiss."

"You're on."

Soon our arms were wrapped around each other. Whatever was on TV, and my mother's opinions on hammocks, the news anchor's blather about an earlier traffic snarl-up in Jamaica Plain, and whatever Tess wanted to gossip about—none of it mattered at all. Only Kevin and me, and the soft couch below, the warm blanket above.

"Hey, seriously. Don't fall asleep," I said when his sleepy eyes closed.

"Same mistake twice," he murmured.

"Yeah, not," I said, beside him.

Then Mom was whispering my name. I opened my eyes. Not my room, living room. I was asleep on the couch. Mmmm. Mom smelled like white wine and fresh air. For a few seconds, I just breathed in the beauty and comfort of her, my eyes blurring her pretty face.

"Charlie," she whispered again. I rested against the sound

of my name in her voice as she pushed my hair off my forehead gently, like she used to when I was little and woke up in the car at night, having arrived somewhere.

"Mmm," I said.

"I'll walk you up," she whispered. "Joe's already upstairs, taking a shower."

"Who?"

"Oh, Charlie." Her chuckle might be my favorite sound in the world, especially when I am sleepy and off-balance.

I jolted awake and looked around. Kevin wasn't there. It was just me and my mother. Maybe the whole thing had been a dream. "Mom."

"Come on." Her arm was around my shoulders as we walked up the stairs together.

"Joe . . . your husband."

Mom laughed. "Yup."

"I thought maybe it was all a dream."

"Sometimes it feels like that to me, too," Mom said. "But no. It's real. Come on, no, don't sit on the steps. Up to bed."

"Where's—was—are Kevin and Samantha already in bed?"

"Yes," Mom said. "Only my rascal stayed up to fall asleep in front of the TV."

I pretended to scowl at her, to cover my smile of relief that at least Kevin had dashed upstairs. Though why hadn't he woken me up, when he ran? My pretend scowl morphed into a real one. "Why is your husband in the shower?"

"He likes to shower before bed," Mom whispered.

"That's just odd."

She giggled a tiny bit, conspiratorially. Like I was her best friend, and we were gossiping about a boy a grade above us.

"Maybe you should trade him in," I suggested.

"You think?"

"Not often," I said.

Mom giggled as if I had come up with that bit of wit on the spot. At the door of her room, with the shower water cascading loudly in the bathroom and, I swear, the sound of her husband singing "Wonderful Tonight," off-key and exuberant, Mom turned to me. "Well, good night," she said.

I had to walk the rest of the way to my room alone, trudging past the dark other bedrooms with their slightly open doors.

twenty-three

WHEN I GOT down to the kitchen in the morning, Samantha was sitting at the table alone, looking glum.

"What's wrong, Sam?"

"They're fighting."

"Who?"

"The parents." She closed her eyes and kept them closed. "Already. Fighting."

"My mom and your dad? No way. The lovebirds?"

She nodded, and one tear leaked out onto her pale, smooth cheek.

"Where are they?"

"Outside." She opened her huge eyes then and stared at me, her mouth curving into a frown. "If they get divorced . . ."

"They're not getting divorced, Sam."

"You didn't hear them. Kevin went back to sleep, to get away from them."

I pulled out a chair and sat across from her at the table. "What did they say?"

She swallowed hard and didn't answer.

"The hammock?"

Sam nodded, crying. Her cheeks blotched up, and her nose started dripping. Oh, girl of my heart—an ugly crier like me.

"So, grilled cheese for breakfast?" I asked, eyeing her barely touched non-breakfast-food breakfast. "You gonna eat that whole thing?" I asked.

She pushed the plate toward me. I picked up half of the sandwich. It had been cut diagonally, the way I like it best, and it had clearly been actually grilled, rather than just heated up. I took a bite.

"Mmmm! This is SO good," I told her, my mouth still half-full.

"It's the thing my dad is out-of-proportion proud of."

"Out-of-proportion proud of? Meaning? Yum."

"Everybody has something," she said, eyes downcast, sniffling in the nose goo. "That's my dad's theory anyway. Something you are way prouder of than the thing deserves. Like, I'm proud of doing well in school, but that's a normal thing. That's in proportion. I am out-of-proportion proud of how good I am at blowing bubbles."

"Gum? Or, like, soapy?"

"Gum," she said. "Bubble gum is my favorite food. And I

can blow excellent bubbles."

"Cool. Was never good at blowing them, myself."

"I could teach you sometime."

"I'd like that," I told her.

"Your mom is out-of-proportion proud of her parallel parking."

I almost drooled grilled cheese out of my mouth, I was laughing so unexpectedly. "That's true!" I said when I eventually regained control of my mouth. "She totally is! She is so freaking proud of how well she parallel . . . how did you know that?"

"She mentions it," Samantha said. "Often. Any time we're in the car with her. She is obviously a very accomplished person, but the only thing I have ever heard her brag about is—"

"Parallel parking!" I finished for her. "You are totally right!"

I guess I was grinning at her, because she was looking at my mouth, and she smiled shyly back at me. I nudged the plate toward her again. "I think your dad might be in proportion with this, though. It's epic. Eat that. Share it with me. It's even better that way."

She slowly picked up the second half and bit off a millimeter, then, weirdly enough, chewed it, before asking me, "What about you?"

"Me?"

"Yes," Samantha said. "What are you proud of, out of proportion to its worth?"

"Hmmm." I put down the last corner of my half of grilled cheese sandwich to think. "I'm pretty good at humiliating myself."

"Not something negative," she said. "Something you are actually proud of."

I thought again. "Losing my phone? No, negative. Ummm . . ."

"You can tell me," Samantha said. "I think I know already."

"What is it? Can you tell me?"

"It doesn't really matter what I think you're disproportionately proud of. You're the one who has to be proud of it."

"Maybe if you tell me, I'll start being proud!"

"Oh, Charlie."

"What's Kevin's thing?"

Samantha smiled. "His is pretty funny. He can—"

The back door slammed. We both turned toward it. Mom dashed across the kitchen to the stairs. The door opened again. Joe, his eyes drooping down in the outside corners where normally they crinkle up, dashed by us, in Mom's footprints.

"Elizabeth," he called after her. "Come on."

He followed her up the stairs.

Samantha and I sat at the table in silence, our unfinished portions of grilled cheese rapidly cooling on the plate between us.

"People argue," I whispered.

"She was crying," Samantha said.

"People cry."

She nodded.

"Hey," I said. "People forgive, too."

"Not really," she said. "They pretend to, but really they don't forgive."

I wanted to argue with her. But her words hit me like a punch in the nose, so I was unable to operate my mouth. Was that true? They pretend to but don't really forgive? And what if you blow off their phone calls and texts and don't even open up your email or Facebook all weekend, just take a vacation from everybody but your own weird, romantic, intense family for one weekend? Would a friend pretend to forgive again? Or was it too late for that, for me and Tess now, too? Was it all just pretending, this reconnecting?

Samantha watched me for a moment and then stood up in her solemn, graceful way and carried her plate to the sink. "He can name all the presidents in order, in under a minute."

"Huh?" I managed. "Who?"

"Kevin. That's his thing. One of his two things."

"Is the other his drawings?" I asked. "Because I think he should be really—"

"No," Samantha cut me off. "That's proportional. The other is, well, do you have a crush on him?"

I felt my face turn bright red, faster than ever before. "No!"

"Yeah, I thought so. He does that, to girls. I'm gonna go up to my room and read now."

"Samantha," I called to her back. She stopped.

I looked at her hair, knotty in two spots and raggedly

uneven in the back, and felt a wave of tenderness crash over me.

"Sometimes people make up," I told her. "They fight, they're mad, and then, sometimes, they move on."

"Yeah," she said. "They move on."

"And sometimes," I said, "seriously, Samantha, I think sometimes they really do forgive."

She stayed still for a few breaths, letting that thought sink down on her, and on me. Then she went upstairs, leaving me to marinate in wonder all alone about whether anything I'd just said was true.

twenty-four

I BROUGHT THE water to a boil. Anya told me to pour about a half cup into the teapot and slosh it around.

"No tea leaves?"

"Not yet," Anya said. "I know Penelope doesn't believe me, but tea is going to be bigger than coffee within a year and we have to be ahead of the curve. This is the magic that is going to get us out of debt, I swear it. I'm not gonna lose this place, if tea catches on."

Penelope and I made eye contact. She looked away first.

"Are you—is there a financial problem?"

"Always," Anya said. "But tea is going to save us. Now pour it out."

I poured the steaming water down the drain. "Why did I do that?"

"You have to warm up the pot first."

"Okay," I said. "Why?"

"So as not to shock the tea," Anya explained, handing me a beige sleeve with loose tea leaves spooned into it.

I placed the sleeve in the warmed pot and poured boiling water over it, with Anya watching. "Wouldn't want to shock the tea," I said.

"Life is shocking enough."

"Absolutely." I almost hugged Anya for that image, of the tea being all shocked, the way I so often am. I couldn't help appreciating how kind it is to warm the teapot to protect the tea from such an experience.

"And then you wait while it steeps," Anya said, wrapping a clean towel around the teapot like a swaddled, much-loved baby. "Four minutes. Then throw away the bag of tea leaves. Got it?"

Ten minutes later, I was leaning against the shiny, clean counter sipping my deliciously un-shocked cup of English Breakfast with milk but no sugar. Anya was right; it was completely different from the tasteless, sad versions of tea I'd ever had before. I held the mug with both hands, warmed inside and out, and put thoughts of angry Tess, squabbling adults, and solemn Sam out of my mind. I closed my eyes and thought about coming out of the shower, before work, and seeing the fogged mirror. *Cool space* was written there, invisible without the steam, but then revealed like a secret message to me, standing damp and charmed in my towel.

I had wiped it clean with one swipe of my hand. But, sipping Anya's warm, magic tea, I promised myself the memory would never be erased from my mind.

It's written in Sharpie on my heart, I was thinking, when Tess slammed open the door of Cuppa.

She glared at me and said, "There you are!"

"Uh-oh," Penelope said beside me, without moving her lips.

I forced myself to smile. "Hi! Hi, Tess."

"What are you good at making?" Tess asked me when she got to the counter.

"A mess," I said.

"True," Penelope agreed, not budging to let me talk privately with Tess. Tess flicked her eyes at Penelope and then back to me. I microshrugged in response.

"Well, if I order a latte or something, can you give me an employee discount?"

"No," Penelope answered.

"I was just kidding," Tess said, and turned back to me. Still hadn't smiled. "Where the heck have you been all weekend?"

"Nowhere," I said, hating the quiver in my voice. "Home."

"Not answering your phone. Not online. What were you doing that you couldn't even . . ."

"I lost my phone and . . ."

"Can you take a break? I have to tell you something."

I looked at Penelope. "Not really," she said.

I looked back and forth between them.

"It's important," Tess said. "I've been calling and texting you all weekend."

"What happened? Tess, is everything okay?"

"It's not like you're being overwhelmed with business. Please? Five minutes."

"Please?" I asked Penelope. "I'll take your turn cleaning the bathroom."

"Men's room."

"Yuck," I said. "Deal. Thanks, seriously, Penelope."

"Toilet, too," Penelope answered.

"Vanilla bean java shake," Tess said. "With extra whipped cream."

"Whoa," I said. "What happened?"

As Penelope went to make the shake, I leaned forward across the bar.

"It's . . . listen," Tess whispered. "I've been trying to get you all weekend. You disappeared."

"Sorry. Is everything okay? Your parents?"

"Nothing like that."

After Penelope handed her the drink and Tess paid, the two of us dashed to our table.

"Five minutes, max," Penelope said to our backs.

"Not Max," I called back. "Charlie."

"And the urinal!" Penelope yelled.

I blew a kiss back at her, then whispered to Tess, "What's wrong?"

"That girl is so weird," Tess whispered back. "Can't believe

177

you have to work with her."

"Penelope? She's awesome. She hates me. I love her."

"You're weird, too."

"True," I admitted. "Tell me."

"Don't be mad," Tess started, then took a long suck on her straw while I tried not to freak out. I hate being told not to get mad. Nobody tells you not to be mad unless she is about to tell you something that would obviously make you mad.

"What?" I tried to be patient while she sipped. "Tess, what?"

"Well, I don't know your current status with Kevin, so I don't want to upset you."

"My current *status*?" She knew. I was screwed. I had no plan. She knew. Obviously she knew. Damn.

"Yeah." She blinked twice, looking down at the table. "I mean, obviously he lives in your house, but are you, like, best friends with him now or something? Because . . ."

Wait. Best friends?

"What? No."

"Seems like you only want to be with him, these days. Inside jokes, and then you go fully off the grid . . ."

"Tess," I said, laying my hand lightly on top of hers the way my mom had done to me in the Thai restaurant. "*You're* my best friend."

"Well," Tess said, with the half shrug, half eye-roll that meant *Not so sure that's true, but anyway.*

"You know you are. Since third grade. My best friend."

"We're a bit old to be talking about who's our best friend, like we're still in Brownies."

I willed myself not to burn up with humiliation at my own immaturity.

"That's not the point, obviously," she quickly continued. "I was talking about Felicity."

"You were?"

Over behind the counter, Penelope cleared her throat at me. A line of people had queued up while I was sitting with Tess. Penelope was dealing all on her own, back there. I should have at least been running the cash register, it was clear.

"I gotta go, Tess," I told her.

"I guess it can wait," she said. "What I had to tell you."

"No, just—tell me quick."

Toby sludged into Cuppa, assessing the room through his heavy-lidded eyes. When he saw me, he lifted his chin slightly in greeting, then smirked toward Penelope, saying "S'up." I was screwing up, and now the only two workers at Cuppa other than me were aware of it. Any second Anya would reappear and, rightly, fire me.

"Who's that?" Tess whispered. "He's kind of hot."

"Nobody. Toby. He's nice. So what did you want—"

"Just I think we should warn Felicity."

"About what?"

"Kevin."

"Kevin? What about—"

"That Kevin is more trouble than she realizes."

"What makes you think Felicity and Kevin—"

"Friday night."

"Friday . . . What happened Friday night?" I asked. "Friday night Kevin was at Brad's."

"This is what I mean."

"What about Felicity?"

"Don't get mad."

"Tess! What would I possibly be mad about?" I could feel my eyes bugging out of my head, my face becoming the poster of every definition of madness. "I'm not mad!"

"We were sleeping over at her house, Felicity's, a few of us—it was already planned before you and I made up, so don't be insulted."

That's what she thought I would be mad about?

Wait, okay, that did make me kind of mad. They were planning to come have a sleepover at my house Saturday after a sleepover Friday at Felicity's that I wasn't invited to? And that would not be awkward because . . . what?

"I knew you were going to take it the wrong way."

"I didn't say—"

"Yeah, Charlie. Subtle is definitely your middle name."

"My parents were going through a weird stage back when they named me, not my fault," I joked back lamely, to show I was still marginally sane even though in fact I might not have been. "And I'm, you know, made of explosions, so . . ."

"Well, anyway, it's so not the point, but you know Felicity's mom is strict about how many people she's allowed to have over, so she couldn't invite you even after I told her everything was resolved between us. Though as it turns out, Darlene couldn't come because she was grounded for smoking, so you probably could've been invited at the last minute, but—"

Anya opened the door to Cuppa, saw the long line and just Penelope behind the bar, hustling as fast as she could go to help people while I sat lollygagging at a table with Tess, and Toby was nowhere to be seen, in the back or the uncleaned bathroom or something.

"Tess, I gotta—"

"Fine, but can you let me say what I needed to tell you?"

"There's more?"

She leaned close and whispered to me, "Kevin and Brad snuck over, and we were playing flashlight tag, right? But then, right in front of us, or, actually, behind that big tree— you know that tree in Felicity's backyard? It's like a big pine tree or something?"

"Hemlock," I said. "Yeah?"

"Hemlock? Isn't that what Socrates took to kill himself?"

"Him and me both, maybe, but anyway, behind the hemlock *what*?"

Tess leaned in toward me again, like she was going to pass the gum in her mouth directly into mine. I could smell it in all its mintiness. Who drinks a vanilla bean java shake and chews peppermint gum at the same time? Only Tess. "Felicity and Kevin were, you know . . ."

"Were what?"

"Well, obviously you can guess. So I just think we ought to warn her, out of friendship, that no matter what he says that sounds so convincing and so romantic, we've both been there and, you know . . . we're like the world's two great experts on the crappiness of Kevin Lazarus."

"Felicity and Kevin hooked up?"

"Congratulations, Sherlock. And what do you want to bet he twirled her hair while they were talking? Did he ever do that to you? Whoa, Nellie, I can tell by your face he did. Right? I know you have to live with him and get along, and you deny it, but you're getting all tight with him. Still—let's be honest. That boy is a total slut! The fact is, Kevin makes girls think he's so madly in love with them, and meanwhile he's off—"

"Charlie?" Anya interrupted, standing over me. "Everything okay?"

I looked up at her, not at all okay. "Yes," I lied. "Sorry. I just . . ."

Anya smiled. "Looks like we could use some help at the counter."

I nodded and stood up.

"Call me later," Tess said, leaving.

I honestly have only the vaguest idea what happened in the next hour and a half. It felt like I was moving in slow motion through scalding water, shocked as tea leaves in an unprepared pot.

twenty-five

WHEN I WALKED into the house, Kevin was alone in the kitchen, his arms pretzeled across his chest and his face dead serious, as if he had been anticipating the fight I was bringing in the door, though when he saw me, his face brightened instantly. Damn that sexy smile of his; it wasn't obliterating my resolve this time.

"Who the hell do you think you are?" I demanded.

His eyebrows crunched together as he squinted at me.

"You've just been playing with me? Is this some kind of sick—"

Samantha skidded into the kitchen in her socks. Her hair was all mussed up, her face blotchy and swollen from crying. "I mean it! Where is he?" Samantha demanded of Kevin.

He looked between me and Sam, uncrossed his arms, and

shrugged his surrender. "You're both crazy. All you people are crazy."

"You people?" I asked. "*You people* as in *girls*?"

"What did you do with him?" Sam screamed as I was saying, "That is rude! And I am not crazy! Tess told me what happened Friday night, and—"

"He was NOT DEAD!" Sam screamed.

"Sam," Kevin said softly.

"Murderer!" She was pointing at Kevin, her eyes bugging out, her face reddening even more. "Killer! Where did you put his body?"

"Stop it, Sam," Kevin said, trying to collect her into a hug, but she was not having any of it; she was rabid, flailing, screaming, and crying.

"Murderer! Killer!"

"Sam, come on," Kevin was cooing in between shooting me nasty looks. "He died. It's okay. It happens."

"You killed somebody?" I asked him.

"Shut up, Charlie."

"Stop telling her to shut up!" Sam screamed. "You always tell her to shut up, and she does not have to shut up, you murderer! Where is the body, you criminal?"

"Sam," Kevin said, blocking his face from her barrage of fists and flails.

"Yeah," I said. "Why do you always tell me to shut up?"

"Because you won't ever frigging shut up!" Kevin yelled. "I flushed him, Sam."

"You FLUSHED HIM?!"

"He's gone."

"DOWN THE TOILET?"

"I—yes. He died. It's like, down the pipes. That's . . ."

"We could have buried him, if he died, which he didn't!"

"A fish should not be buried, Sam. He's a water animal."

"Your fish died?" I asked her. Oh, her fish. Poor thing.

"No!" she screamed.

"Oh," I said.

"Yeah, he did," Kevin said, impatience sneaking into his quiet voice. "He died. He had some sort of mold starting to grow out of his side, Sam."

"That wasn't mold! It was—he was—sometimes a fish—"

"And he was starting to smell bad," Kevin said. "You can't leave a dead fish decomposing for so long."

"He was sleeping!" Sam wailed, and then, as if all her bones liquefied at once, she melted down onto the floor, weeping.

"Oh, Sam," I tried. "I'm sorry. I know you really cared about that fish."

"Alpha," she sobbed.

Kevin wrapped his arms around shaking Sam on my kitchen floor and started singing the word *okay,* over and over again to her, into her tangled hair.

Not knowing what else to do, and seeing that my own argument with Kevin was going to have to wait in line, I went and got a Diet Pepsi out of the fridge. I popped it open and sat at the counter, trying to be inconspicuous. Also trying to

185

maintain my rage at what a jerk Kevin was, despite the fact that he was singing a soothing song, the only lyrics of which were *okay*, into his distraught little sister's hair.

My phone was there, beside the sink. Hmm.

"It's my fault," Samantha was sobbing. "My fault my fault my fault."

"No," Kevin said. "No."

"I shouldn't have . . ."

"You didn't do anything wrong," he said. "You didn't. Fish die. Betta fish die fast."

"The last one lasted a YEAR!" she sobbed.

"Well, see?" He wiped her tears off her blotchy cheeks. Day-ummm. "You're really amazingly good with fish. Maybe this guy was a very old fish when you got him. Or had some kind of medical condition it was born with. You can't know. It was NOT your fault."

Samantha sniffled hard, then flicked her eyes up to me and said, "My fish died."

"I heard," I said.

"And Kevin flushed him down the toilet."

Ah, just like he did with my life, I thought, but instead I said, "I'm so sorry, Sam."

"I loved him," Sam said, and started sobbing again. "I loved Alpha!"

"Everything that lives, dies," Kevin said.

Sam stiffened, suddenly still, not breathing. Then, fast as a prizefighter, she cocked back her tiny right arm and clocked

Kevin hard across the jaw with her tight fist.

He was still toppling backward when she sprinted from the room. I watched him rubbing the bottom of his face as her fast footsteps tapped up the stairs out of sight. When the house had descended into its old silence, Kevin turned to me and said, "Good thing I lied about flushing him."

"You . . . lied?"

"I put him down the garbage disposal."

"You—but—that's awful!"

"Shhh." He stood up, still rubbing his jaw. "I got your phone for you, from the shed."

"Holy crap! Down the . . . really?"

"There was so much water, I thought it might swamp the toilet. I kept texting you for advice, but . . ."

"I was at work. And my phone was . . ."

"Yeah, I know. I found it for you after. But nobody else was around," Kevin whispered fiercely. "My dad and your mom have been out for hours, making up about the damn hammock. Sam got all stressed out when they were fighting and then her tooth falling out, so she went down to throw rocks in the lake, and I saw the fish, floating . . ."

"Her tooth fell out?"

"Yeah, big day around here. You missed a lot of fun. So on top of everything, I didn't want to flood the toilet and then there'd be a dead fish and who knows what else flooding the house. And then your mom would get mad at me, too, and . . ."

"My mom doesn't really get mad."

"No? Okay."

"Maybe *your* mom gets mad. I don't know. Not mine."

"Shut the hell up, Charlie."

"Fine," I said. "I don't care." I pushed the image of him all sweet and gentle huddled over his sobbing sister from my mind, letting the other one replace it—the image I had been unable to shake all day, of him laughing with Felicity in the dark, grabbing her by her waist in the dark, thinking they were unseen just because they were making out behind that big hemlock in her backyard. . . . "I don't care about any of it. Including anything you do."

"Chuck," he said. "I don't—I'm sorry. Okay? I just don't like to talk about my—"

"About what? About how many girls you're hooking up with at a time?"

"What?" He gave me his oh-so-innocent face, all perplexed and cutely confused.

"I know," I said, and stood up. The Diet Pepsi was too sweet, too bubbly, and I was feeling neither sweet nor bubbly myself. "I know all about Friday night."

"Friday night."

"Yeah. You and Brad, at Felicity's? Look, spare me the innocent routine you use on your father, okay? I'm not even asking *what* you did or *if* you did it, because I already know!"

"Okay," he said. "I don't know what you think you know, but, okay."

"It's not okay!" I yelled. "What did you, like, tell Brad, 'Hey, check it out, I can hook up all night with Charlie because, what the hell, she's so convenient, and then I can get with Felicity, too'?"

"You. Are. Nuts," he said, his hands up in front of his chest.

"I'm not nuts!" I screamed. Non-nuttily. Maybe. "May as well flush ME down the toilet, too. Or toss me in the garbage disposal, why don't you?"

He stepped so close to me we were nose-to-nose, like we'd been so often recently, but now with a way different emotion charging the inch between us. "Samantha has really good hearing, so shut the hell up."

"Stop telling me to shut up!" I yelled.

"Charlie," he growled, indicating upstairs with the slightest incline of his head.

"Oh, now you're embarrassed?" I asked in a slightly quieter voice. I could feel myself right at the edge of completely losing it, holding myself back by the weakest thread. "That your little sister might know what a jerk you are to girls?"

His jaw clenched and reclenched.

"That she might think it's okay to let boys treat her the way you treat me?"

"Stop," Kevin growled.

"Bet Brad thinks you're such the stud, huh? What did you tell him about me?"

"Nothing," Kevin said. "And why would you even care?

189

Brad? What the hell—is this all from Tess? Why do you even listen to her? She has never been a decent friend to you and you know it, but you still chase after her, believing everything she says, doing anything she wants."

"You know what, Kevin? This isn't about me and Tess."

"No?"

"No! You want to hook up with Felicity? That's fine. I don't care. Just don't lie to me."

"I never lied to—"

"Yeah, you did," I snapped. "We weren't officially—anything. True. 'Undefined,' you wanted. Yeah. I get it. I didn't then, obviously, but now I do. My fault, I'm so gullible—I thought that 'cool space' you talked about was, well, cool! Or hot! Or some other excellent temperature thing. And by the way, it wasn't Gandhi who said, 'The time to make up your mind about people is never.' It's from an old movie called *The Philadelphia Story*. Katharine Hepburn, not Gandhi."

"Okay."

"I get it now," I said, on a roll. "Why you wanted it like that—all the fun, none of the limits. No strings. Great. I guess I signed up for that, fine, my bad. But be honest at least to yourself, Kevin. You were lying to me every time you looked at me, or touched me, or kissed me. Every time you made me feel like I was—*something*—to you."

He shook his head. "Whatever."

"Whatever?" I was shaking.

He started walking away.

"I trusted you," I said to his back.

"Yeah," he said. "Right back at you."

And then he was gone.

twenty-six

"YOU OKAY?" MOM asked, poking her head into my room.

"Yeah," I said. "You?"

She nodded, then shrugged. "Overreacted. Apologized."

"I mean, a hammock. Why do people think that's nice?"

She sat down on the edge of my bed. "They just make me seasick."

"No, but I mean, what is a hammock supposed to symbolize, or not symbolize, but . . ."

We heard Joe knocking on Kevin's door, a sound I knew too well from the other side of it. "Kev?"

"Go away!" Kevin yelled.

"I should go," Mom whispered. "Work was good today?"

"Yeah."

Kevin's door squeaked open, then clicked closed.

Mom went to my door. "Everything else is good?"

"Dandy," I said, and she left.

All I could hear after that was the low murmur of Joe's voice, and the occasional "NO" from Kevin.

One time when I was little, during a playdate at Tess's house, we got in big trouble. We'd taken her mom's jewelry box into Tess's closet and were playing with all the tinkly, sparkling things. The moment Tess's closet door was opened, I almost peed in my pants. We'd been Russian royalty on the run, in the dark Siberian wilderness of her closet floor, but with Tess's mom staring down at us, we were just two naughty little girls. I'd never been in trouble with somebody else's mom before. After the necklaces, bracelets, and rings that Tess had put on me were removed by her mother, I was sent down to the living room while Tess and her mom had a "private talk." I remember sitting there, my feet dangling off the chintz couch, listening to her mother's angry voice. I felt small, terrified, embarrassed, and guilty; I remember wishing I could magically teleport away from that scratchy couch to home, where everything would be okay.

Same thing, overhearing Kevin and his father now—except that I was already home. Where could I teleport to?

I heard pencils skittering across his floor and then a shattering thud. I froze, thinking, *Did he just punch a hole in the wall?*

In my old life, there was just Mom and me. Sometimes

when we got really crabby with each other (not very often), one of us would stomp away and flop down poutily in a chair to read. Within an hour, we'd get over it and eat some ice cream on the deck together.

Nobody ever took it out on a canister of pencils, and definitely nobody's fist went through anything. Until, possibly, this.

I was trapped in my room, pressed against the wall with my heart pounding like a sprinter's. Because what if I decided to leave my room at the same moment either Kevin or his dad stormed out of Kevin's room? There would be a horribly awkward traffic jam, rounding the corner toward the stairs, and maybe flying writing implements, which could be—

"Get out," Kevin growled.

Murmur, murmur from Joe.

"I hate her!"

He hates *her*? Who's *her*? My mother? Samantha? Me? *He has no right to hate me,* I thought. *Her* better not be *me*.

His door opened and closed again. Footsteps on the stairs. Whose? I couldn't tell the difference yet between Kevin's stomping and his father's.

I wish Tess were here, I thought, and then dashed across my room to grab my phone and text her.

Kevin just I think punched a hole in the wall of his room.

Which is his room? Tess texted back in one second.

Guest room/not rly the point!

Becuz you told him not to be a jerk to Felicity?

194

NO. Maybe. IDK. Something with his dad? Then I thought again. *Or maybe his mom? He threw his sister's fish down the garbage disposal.*

Why wd he do THAT?

It was dead, I added quickly. *But still.*

That is bizarre. He's worse than I thought!

I am trapped in my room! What if I have to go to the bathroom sometime in the next few years while he is still living here?

I guess you'll have to try to hold it in, Tess texted back. *Only three years to go.*

Thanks tons, I texted back, though in fact it did kind of help. So I added, *I am not sure my mom thought this whole thing through, when she decided we could handle having External Americans living in the same house as us.*

Tess texted: *<3 <3 <3.*

So at least there was that.

twenty-seven

I SET MY alarm for 5:55, my luckiest time, and when I woke up to it I didn't even hit snooze but instead went down to the blessedly empty kitchen to have a bowl of cereal all by myself while I finished up my homework. Then I went up, took a quick shower, and saw nothing revealed in the foggy mirror.

Just fog.

I remembered that Sam had lost her tooth.

After I dried off most of the way and got damply dressed, I tiptoed into her room and slipped a dollar under her pillow. She was sleeping flat on her back, like a pretend kid—or a corpse—one hand on her stomach and one on her heart, a small, pretty smile on her pink lips. I just stood there looking at her for a minute. The dollar I'd put under there was from the first money I'd ever earned outright on my own, not a gift from a relative or a bribe from my father. It was from my share of the tip jar from the day before, shoved into my pocket with my numb hand before I'd hurled myself toward home to the Kevin disaster show.

I hadn't even gotten to enjoy the fact of having made my own money yet. But I did enjoy it, standing there watching Sam sleep. There was obviously a lot going on, but a kid should get a buck from the tooth fairy anyway. It felt grown-up to be the one slipping it under the pillow.

When I turned around, Kevin was standing in her doorway in his jeans with no shirt or socks on. He stepped aside as I passed, his mouth a straight, tight line.

I slipped out of the house just as people were starting to clomp around upstairs, leaving a note saying I had an early meeting at school, so I was riding my bike there.

I got my own bike out of the shed and rode as fast as possible, outracing my thoughts. The tires were a little flat, so it was more of a workout than I'd intended. Should've borrowed Kevin's . . . Damn, every thought led inevitably back to Kevin. No, stop it. I pumped the pedals faster. My bike, my own, my freedom. At school I locked up next to Tess's bike and texted her on my way in.

Where r u? Am here (@school) early.

Come to my locker! she immediately texted back, as I knew she would. Her house is such a hot mess in the mornings—she always rides to school and gets there before the doors open.

She was sitting with her excellent posture straight up

against her locker when I got there, her legs splayed wide in front of her. She gave me her awesome full-face smile, and I just slumped down next to her.

She put her arm around me. "Wanna run away from home?"

"Yes," I said, my head lolling onto her shoulder. "Will you come with me?"

"Of course! We'll have adventures. Live off the land. Suck the marrow out of life."

"Ew."

"True. Suck the goo out of the chocolates."

"And leave all the bad ones in the box."

"Absolutely," she said.

People were stepping over us, so we stood up. "I hate Kevin," I said.

"We should make it a club," she responded. "We could get jackets. Maybe a theme song."

"I hate Kevin," I sang. "I truly hate his guts."

"I hate Kevin," she sang, same tune. "Such a frigging slut."

I grinned at her and she grinned back, my almost twin, my double, my best friend. "We might have to work on the theme song a bit."

"I hate Kevin," she sang as we started off toward homeroom. "He grinds fishes in the disposal."

"I hate Kevin," I sang, thinking fast. "He blinds girls-es with his—mind-control-sal."

Tess squealed. "You are sooo random."

We giggled and blew each other kisses good-bye.

Later, in science class, we had to present our project ideas. I felt Kevin's eyes on me when I stood up front, reading from my paper about my plans to test the five-second rule by dropping gummi bears on various floors for one second, five seconds, ten seconds, and twenty seconds, swab them for bacteria, and then compare with undropped gummi bears as a control.

Everybody laughed and made predictions. Except Kevin.

When he had to go up, I kept my eyes on my desk until he was in the midst of detailing his proposal. He was planning to test bathrooms—in the school, in the house he was living in (he didn't say *in my house*; he said *in the house I am living in*), in a coffee shop, in a McDonald's—and compare to see which is the grossest.

I could feel kids in the class turning to see my reaction. I tried to stay neutral, but I'm sorry, WHAT? He was going to swab my bathroom to see if it was as gross as the school bathroom or a fast-food restaurant's or, what? The men's room at Cuppa? To see if it was gross? And then put his results on a damn piece of poster board?

Mrs. Roderick said, "Oh, sounds like you and Charlie have similar ideas. Maybe you'll team up?"

"No," we both answered.

"Well," Mrs. Roderick said, blinking her long, fake eyelashes at us. One of them was only partially attached, giving her a kind of kooky, unsettling look. "That was unanimous. Okeydokey. Next?"

Kevin passed my seat, going back to his.

I sank down and waited for time to slog by. At the end of class, Tess was at my side before the bell finished ringing. On our way out the door, she whispered to me, "You know what's weird? For a few days there, I was all worried you were ditching me for Kevin. I was all like, *Charlie is totally getting back at me, making me feel jealous as revenge for all those times she felt jealous of me.*"

"Really?"

"Crazy, right? But I can see now how jealousy can make a person do crazy stuff, and anyway, I'm over it because I see you love me way more than that boy-slut."

"Um," I said. "Good, I guess?"

"I love love love your science fair project. Let's figure out a way we can combine it with mine. More fun that way. Hey, did you know *funeral* is an anagram of *real fun?*"

I had to laugh. "That is the most awesome thing ever."

I walked home by myself after school.

At least Kevin hadn't quit newspaper, like I had, or maybe he was at baseball. I wasn't memorizing his schedule anymore.

I had a ton of homework, and it probably meant nothing that Anya hadn't called me about when to come in for my first official day yet. She had said it might be a few days. Anyway, I was very busy, so it was just as well. I had many hobbies of my own, buried deep down, to get busy developing.

Sam was sitting on the landing midway up the stairs, reading a book.

"Hey, Sam," I said. "How's it going?"

"Great," she said. "I'm going to buy bubble gum with the money I got from the tooth fairy. I usually get a dollar, but this time I got four."

"Really?" I asked. "Four? Wow."

"I know," Sam said. "Strange coincidence, right? My dad is going to take me to buy the gum, and I will be happy to teach you bubbles tonight, if you're free."

"I'll look forward to that," I said.

I took a short break on my bed when I got there. I wished I could be more like Sam, able, still, to just lose myself sprawled on a step, reading a book. Or like Mom, in love, successful in a career, settled with everything. Or like Joe, artistic and generous. Even maybe like my dad, certain of everything.

Dad.

I scrolled through my emergency contacts. How had I not thought of this before?

"Dad?" I said into the phone when he picked up. "Hi!"

"Who is this?" my father asked.

"It's your kid, the older one, the one from your first marriage," I said, aware of the edge of sarcasm mixed with about-to-cry in my voice that I had sworn to myself only thirty seconds earlier I could avoid. "It's Charlie, Dad."

"Charlotte!" he said. "How are you? Everything okay?"

"Yeah, Dad, sure," I told him.

"Your mother's fine?"

"Yeah."

"Jim treating her okay?"

"Joe," I said. "I just wanted to ask you if . . ."

"What? I can't hear you. Why are you sniveling?"

"Allergies," I said, and immediately regretted it. He thinks having allergies is, like sniveling, a sign of a weak character. "Or, nothing. Dad? Would it be okay with you if . . ."

"Charlotte, honey, I just got home from work, and I have to get out to the yard or I'll never—"

"Okay, but, Dad? You're going to Paris over spring break?"

"Yeah," he said. "Gotta get some French fries. Hahaha."

"But what about me?" My face in my mirror looked so pathetic I sank down on the far side of my bed and closed my eyes, waiting.

"It's extremely expensive, Charlotte."

"I know," I said.

"I can't bankroll your every wish, you know."

"I know. I wasn't asking to come to Paris with you. . . ."

"Yup. You keeping your grades up?"

"Yeah. Dad. Maybe I could just come for a visit. This weekend, even. It's been a while, and ABC must be so big by now. . . ."

"He's still a punk, aren't you, ABC?"

"No," I heard my little half brother say, and then heard my father laugh. ABC, who was almost five and adorable, started to giggle. My father must have been tickling him, from the roller-coaster sound of his giggles—and my father's ragged breath, whispering, "Oh yeah? Oh yeah?"

"Dad?" I considered telling him that Shakespeare used the word *punk* to mean *prostitute*, so maybe he shouldn't call his favorite kid that. But then I didn't. Couldn't.

"Hmmm? Charlotte?"

"Yeah, I'm still here."

"Okay, you take care," Dad said. "Say hello to your mom for me. How's her marriage going? Better this time around?"

"I guess so," I said.

"Well, send her and Jim my best."

"Joe."

"What?"

"Nothing."

"You working yet? Or just lazing around with your nose in a book?"

I hesitated. "You know me," I finally said.

"Honey, you gotta get your ass in gear, huh? Life's not just entertainment."

"Really?"

"Yes, it is," I heard ABC say, through the phone. "For me it is."

My father play-grunted at him. "I'm gonna get you, you punk," he said in a grizzly-bear voice, and then, to me, said, "Gotta go, honey. Talk to you soon."

"Bye, Dad," I said, and hung up before he could.

I threw my phone down on the bed and flung open my

door. Just what I needed—Kevin was on his way to his room, at the same moment. Well, I was not about to slink back into my room just because some jerk-slut punk interloper was clogging up my hall.

"Hey! Kevin!" I whisper-yelled, warning myself not to talk loud enough for Sam to overhear, and further not to say aloud the too-silly-for-how-furious-I-felt word *interloper*.

"What?" He turned around, his arms crossed in front of his chest.

You interloper! "I really didn't appreciate your little science project jab."

"Okay."

"Okay?"

"I really have no idea what you're talking about."

"Right," I said. My arms were crossed in front of my chest, too. "Sure you don't. Your science project is basically a way of insulting my house, you interloper." *Damn.*

"What?" He took a step closer and growled at me, "Not everything is about YOU, believe it or not."

"Screw you. I never said it was."

"Why would you think my project was specifically designed to dis you?"

"Well, you're planning to—what? Swab my bathroom and compare it to every gross place you can find, and see how it stacks up? To broadcast to the entire school how messy my house is? I'm not the one with Head & Shoulders in the shower and my wet towel and dirty underwear on the floor. So, watch where you throw stones, you know? Because I have plenty of ammunition, and you live in MY frigging glass house."

"At least I didn't steal my science project idea from a nine-year-old."

"And I did?"

"Yeah," he said. "You did. I was there. String bean on the floor?"

"You think you people invented the five-second rule? How frigging arrogant are—"

"You're the most arrogant person I—"

At that moment, my mother came up the stairs, a stack of books in her arms and her reading glasses crooked on her nose. "Hi," she said. "Everything okay, you guys?"

"Fine," Kevin and I answered in unison. Then we retreated to our rooms. So much for not getting detoured by the interloper.

twenty-eight

"THE FIVE-SECOND RULE," I told him.

"That is the most excellent science project ever," Toby responded, topping a coffee with a perfect dome of steamed milk. He placed the mug on the counter in front of a grateful, frazzled mom of twin toddlers who were screeching in the stroller beside her, poking each other with gunky fingers.

"Sorry again," I said, because of the time she'd had to waste while I wrecked three tries at making it for her.

She tried to give back an understanding nod, but clearly the full measure of her understanding had been used up on her ogre babies. She steered the stroller to the front corner and faced it to the wall, then slid down in her seat, the warm mug Toby had given her nestled between her palms. She sipped as her eyes closed.

"Never gonna have kids," I whispered to Toby.

"You sound like my mom," he responded.

I was laughing when the door to Cuppa opened. Felicity and Paige walked in, followed closely by Kevin and Brad.

"Friends of yours?" Toby whispered. I guess I had stiffened a little.

I turned my back to them and whispered, "My ex, and his newbie."

"Which?" Toby whispered.

"Blue-eyed boy. And ponytail."

"I got this," he said to me, and then to them, across the counter, "Hey."

"Hi," Felicity said, then turned to Kevin. "Do you know what you want?"

"Yes," Kevin said, glaring at me.

"Ugh, I'm so indecisive," Felicity said. "What are you getting?"

"So?" Toby said to me, leaning his hip against the counter, while my friends discussed the relative merits of Cuppa's various offerings.

"So," I answered.

"So we're on for Saturday night, then?" he asked me.

First I'd heard of it. "Yeah. Sure."

"So cool that you like Apollo Run."

"Are you kidding?" I asked, pretending that was just an expression instead of an honest question. "They're great!" Please let Apollo Run be a THEY.

"Have you heard their new song?" Toby asked.

"The best," I said. "Though, of course, their old stuff . . ."

"Sure." Toby's hand pulled my shoulder close to his armpit. "We'll hang with them after, they'll love you."

The shaking started at my feet and spread upward. No way any of these people in front of the counter, all of whom I'd known since elementary school, would believe I was going to see a band with this senior guy. They had stopped discussing drinks and were all facing us, waiting to order, but Toby was paying attention only to me, completely ignoring them. If Anya walked out of the storeroom, she'd be pissed.

"Sounds great," I said, and turned around to clean the already gleaming machines with my rag while my friends ordered their overly sweet drinks from Toby.

They took their drinks to go. I waved good-bye and even mustered a smile. Kevin was first to walk out and didn't hold the door for anybody. Brad at least turned around and said, "See you back at the ranch!"

Felicity giggled at that and so, therefore, did Paige.

When the door closed behind them, I wilted onto the stool behind the counter, even though Toby was the senior person on and had rights to it.

"Thank you," I said.

"You must do improv," he answered.

"Why?" I asked instead of admitting that no, I never did anything of the kind.

"You're good at it. The rule."

"The rule?"

"'Yes, and.' Whatever your scene partner says, you say yes, and then add . . . You're yanking my chain, aren't you?"

"No," I said. "I mean, yes, and . . ."

"And?"

"And I . . . am secretly an improv pro. You know, in the greater Boston area."

"You don't get out to Chicago much these days?"

I'd never been to Chicago. "Chicago is so done now."

"True that," he said. "And."

"And."

"And it sucks when you have to see your ex with somebody else the first time."

"Yes," I said. "And—it does. And that really helped. And it was fun."

He nodded. "'Twas. Your turn to clean the milk station."

"On it," I said. I made it gleam. Felt good to scrub something clean.

twenty-nine

DESPITE MY EFFORTS to avoid her, Felicity continued being very friendly to me all week at school. She asked me a bit about Toby, and the band we were going to see, and about working at Cuppa. She was being so nice it was hard to avoid falling into a happy friendship with her. But as soon as I felt myself sucked into a conversation, walking down the hall with her or sitting together at lunch, I'd picture her behind that hemlock in her backyard with Kevin's hand tangled in her hair, and my mind would clamp as tight as my jaw.

At those moments, she'd tilt her head a bit, confused, and let it go, wandering off with Paige or one of her other adorable friends. It wasn't fair, I realized—she had no idea I was involved with Kevin when she got hair-tangled in it, and of course I had to keep it that way. She couldn't know. And I of all people had a heck of a nerve being mad at anybody for kissing Kevin while I was (secretly, unofficially) going out with him, after what I had done to Tess knowing full well that she was publicly, officially falling in love with him at the time.

Urgh.

Sometimes it was hard to be friends with myself.

And then, of course, Tess started asking me about Toby. We were getting to be the talk of the school: me and that cool senior, going to see an awesome band Saturday night in Harvard Square. Tess thought I was being humble, saying *I don't know* and *We're just friends from work*.

The fact that Felicity and Tess seemed impressed and Kevin seemed pissed off meant more to me than I wanted to admit. Exactly when I felt least likable, I was hitting my popularity zenith.

Friday afternoon, Tess came over so we could work on our science projects together. We stopped off in town and bought gummies for me and water for her, since she was doing taste tests of bottled water, to see how they ranked on a scale from one to ten. Neither of us were likely to win Nobels, it was clear to us both.

We were in my kitchen dropping gummi bears, counting, and cracking up when Kevin came in from baseball practice.

"Hi, Kevin!" Tess said, turning on her full wattage.

What? Since when was she so friendly to Kevin?

"Will you taste-test these waters?" she asked him.

"Okay," he said. He put down his mitt and sat on the bench his father had placed beside our back doorway. He took off his sneakers while Tess poured a little water from each bottle into a separate cup, then lined up all ten plastic cups beside numbered index cards across the kitchen table, whispering to me the whole time about what I should write down on her pad.

Kevin came to the table and crossed his arms over his chest, wary of her and of the activity, looking down at the plastic cups as if maybe she had put poison in some of them. "What am I supposed to do?"

"Choose one, drink it, and say how much you like it."

He picked up cup number five and drank it like a shot. "So?"

"It's fine."

"On a scale of one to ten."

"It's water," he said.

"Just give it a rating," Tess said. "It's my science project. Come on."

"Maybe taste another and compare them," I suggested.

He chugged cup number one. "It's water, too."

"They're all water," Tess said. "But don't they taste subtly different?"

"No," Kevin said.

"Are you taste-blind, too?"

"Too?"

"Yeah," Tess said. "Color-blind *and* taste-blind?"

He looked at me then, first time all day.

212

"I didn't . . ." There was nothing I could say. Obviously I had told Tess he was color-blind. "You didn't say it was a secret."

He grabbed on to the edge of the table. I stepped back, involuntarily, picturing him flipping over the table and dumping everything.

"We're best friends, Kevin," Tess said. "Charlie tells me everything! Your rocket ship underpants, how you fart if you eat cheese—"

I jumped in: "I never—"

"Just like you told Brad about how Charlie eats cookies in the middle of the night. What do you expect?"

My mouth dropped open. "You told Brad?"

"I didn't," Kevin said.

"I knew it. I can't believe you."

"Me?"

"Would you guys calm down?" Tess laughed. "Come on, Kevin. Just rate the stupid waters so I don't fail science?"

So Kevin sipped each cup of water and rated them. I think he chose random numbers, which I wrote down in Tess's notebook. Then he went upstairs, and Tess and I hung out until it was time for her to go home.

"I see what you mean," she said. "It's, like, tense in your house now. It always used to be so chill here. So, you're really going to Harvard Square with that guy Toby tomorrow night?"

"That's what he said," I didn't lie.

"Well, text me if you need me," she said, buckling her helmet under her chin. "You know, if you suddenly get that *gotta go* feeling."

"I will, thanks." I sat down on my back step. "Hey, Tess?"

"Yeah?" She was already straddling her bike, ready to go.

"From now on, don't, if I tell you something about Kevin, don't . . ."

"You both need to lighten up." She blew me a kiss and flew down the hill on her bike, her long hair streaming out behind her.

thirty

I LET HALF an hour pass after the parents left for dinner with their friends before I went to look for Samantha. She wasn't in the kitchen or the living room, so I pulled myself up the stairs, yanking on the banister. Kevin's door was half-open, but I didn't see him in there. Samantha was on her bed with her eyes closed and a huge, heavy book open on her stomach.

"Hey, Sam," I said. "You okay?"

"Just resting."

"Okay," I said. "You want to teach me how to blow those bubbles?"

"No, thank you," she said.

"Sorry I couldn't rally last night."

"That's okay," she whispered.

I leaned against the door frame and watched her pretty face relax little by little, her eyelashes resting on her pale cheeks.

It was nice.

I could have stayed there for hours—maybe I should have, in hindsight. But instead I turned around and saw that Kevin was standing in the hallway outside Samantha's room, staring at me with those intense, half-closed eyes that are my kryptonite.

I stepped around him and was on my way to my room when he asked, "You really going out with that pothead?"

I turned around, in front of his open door, to face him. "He's not a pothead, and none of your business," I said. "You really going out with that airhead?"

"I thought she's one of your crew," Kevin said, stepping toward me. "Don't you people tell each other everything?"

"I think you got me mixed up with you," I snarled back, not letting myself enjoy the fact that Kevin hadn't denied that his girlfriend or hookup or whatever, Felicity, was an airhead. "How much did you tell Brad about us?"

"I'm not the one who—"

"If you guys are going to fight," Samantha called from inside her dark room, "could you do it downstairs? I'm trying to fall asleep."

"We're done," Kevin called back to her. "Let's not . . ."

"Absolutely," I agreed, crossing my arms over my chest. "Let's not."

"So . . . can I get into my room?"

"Your room."

"Yeah," he said. "Look, I didn't ask to move in here. You don't want me here. But here I am. Right? And I have no frigging out. I have no place I can go to not be here. Or I'd go in a heartbeat. You don't like my shampoo? Well, sorry it's not up to your standards, but honestly? Screw you. I don't want any part of the stupid little dramas you and your friends cook up to torture one another. You want to hook up with every skeezy guy in school, even if he's way too old for you, which he is, by the way? Good. Fine, whatever. Do it. Why should I care? I don't care what you do, or what your conniving friend Tess thinks I did, or your mother's feelings about goddamn hammocks, or my father's stupid rules, or my deadbeat mom's sorry-ass excuses, or the frigging cleanliness of the freaking bathroom! So, for now, yeah. My room. Because I have no damn choice. So how about you take two steps to the side and leave me the hell alone."

"I hate you!" I yelled.

"Right back at you."

"Sam," I said, seeing her emerge at a slant from her room, just the top half of her angling out, disheveled and squinting.

"I . . ." Her eyes were mostly closed.

"Sorry," I told her. "We're done. We were just—everything's okay. Go back to bed. Sam? You okay?"

She was sort of slumping down against her door frame.

"Sam?" I asked, stepping toward her.

"I don't feel so . . . ," she mumbled.

And then she hit the floor in a heap.

thirty-one

SAMANTHA WAS BLUISH-WHITE and limp, a tiny rag doll there on the floor. I took her head onto my lap. She was breathing, but not very much.

"Kevin!"

He was standing above us in a flash. Then he sank down beside us, bluish too, like it was contagious.

"Call nine-one-one," I said.

"I don't, I can't—"

"Now, Kevin," I said. "My phone is right there, by your foot. Grab my phone and call nine-one-one."

"Maybe I should call my mom," he said. "Is she . . . what happened? What's wrong with her?"

"I don't know. Kevin, nine-one-one."

"I didn't, if anything . . ."

I didn't want to bobble Samantha's head, but Kevin was useless, muttering to himself, his head between his knees. I slipped one hand under Samantha's head and reached past Kevin to grab my phone. I pressed the buttons I had never called before, because you never call 911 unless it's a real emergency, or you could get in big trouble or distract them from the real emergencies.

Kevin, meanwhile, was saying, "We better call—I have to call my dad—call my dad first because, if, he's gonna be so mad, so . . . at me, if we . . ."

I stopped listening to him because the operator had picked up.

"I have an emergency," I told her, thinking, *No kidding. Thought you called 911 because you wanted to order a pizza.* "I need an ambulance because there is a nine-year-old who just passed out and she is, she looks like she might be, um, dying."

There's a joke Tess told me last year. Two hunters in the woods, one collapses, the other calls 911 and says, "I'm hunting in the woods with my buddy, and I think he's dead; help!" The operator asks, "Are you sure he's dead?" The hunter says, "Hold on a sec." There's a gunshot, and then the hunter gets back on the phone and says, "Okay, now he's definitely dead. Now what?"

I was answering questions and following directions: giving the 911 lady my address, checking in Sam's mouth to make sure she wasn't choking on anything. I had my finger digging around Sam's wet mouth, but everything was happening in slow enough slow motion to let me have that stupid middle-school joke running through my head at the same time, and berating myself for it on a separate track. My voice, answering the operator, sounded far away and like Mom's—calm, capable, in control: *No, I don't think she ingested any poison, drugs, or alcohol; yes, in fact, she did seem a little ill earlier in the day. Yes, she is still breathing. Yes, I can feel a pulse in her neck, but I don't know how strong a pulse is actually supposed to feel.*

"Yes," I answered. "I'm her . . . her, well, I'm her, uh, step-sister."

"Is there an adult in the house?"

"No, we're babysitting."

"Who's there with you?"

I looked over at Kevin, his face tight and pale with worry, crouched beside us, rocking, bunched up tight.

"It's my, just, he's, we're babysitting—can you just please send an ambulance?"

"It's on the way. Send your boyfriend down to open the front door, honey."

"He's not my . . ." I just hung up. "The ambulance is coming. Kevin? You need to go down and open the front door. Okay? Kevin? Kevin!"

"Charlie, if anything—"

"Now. Go. The front door, Kevin; not the back door. You have to unbolt it. Go. I'll call the parents. She'll be okay. I swear. Trust me."

Kevin nodded and sprang up. I heard him cursing the

220

whole way down the stairs and then flinging the door open. From the distance, sirens approached.

I pushed Samantha's hair back from her forehead and whispered at her, "I just promised Kevin that you would be all right. And I'm done lying. So you better not die."

Without opening, her eyes twitched three times, and then she whispered, "Okay."

"Samantha?"

She didn't respond at all. While I called Mom's phone and silently begged, *Pick up pick up,* I wondered if maybe I had imagined that *Okay.*

"Hello?"

"Mom."

The sirens were right outside already.

"Hey, Charlie," Mom said, the wonderful lightness lilting in her voice. "Everything good there?"

I took a quick breath. "No. Something's wrong with Samantha. You need to come home. Actually, you need to meet us at the hospital."

"What? Joe, something happened to Sam. What happened? What's going on?"

"She collapsed. I called nine-one-one. The ambulance is here. They're on their way up the stairs. They're here. Meet us at the hospital, okay?"

She was talking, and Joe was yelling questions in the background, but I said firmly to her, "I have to go now, Mom. See you at the hospital. Come quick."

I put the phone down because the paramedics were pushing me away. The man was checking Samantha, poking and grabbing at her, slapping her cheeks, asking me questions like if I gave her any drugs. *Drugs? No. I argued with her brother, that is all.* The woman, who was the bigger of the two, started firing questions at me.

"Does she have any medical conditions?"

"Just the lack of consciousness," I answered.

"Before this, wise guy."

"I wasn't trying to be—no. Not that I know of. She's nine."

"Did she fall?"

"Yes."

"Did she hit her head when she fell?"

"No," I said, picturing how she just kind of went boneless, liquefied, not solid flesh—what was that from? Oh yeah, *Hamlet: melt, thaw, and resolve itself into a dew.* "I don't think so. I'm not sure."

Both EMTs froze and stared at me. "Did you see her fall?"

"Yes."

"Get the collar," the woman barked at the man. He dashed down the stairs. They were obviously about to arrest me.

"I'm pretty sure she didn't hit her head," I said. *Collar* is cop-speak for arresting somebody. I definitely saw that on TV. *I swear I wasn't trying to be fresh! It's just a habit, when I'm nervous!*

"Better to be sure," the woman said, I guess to explain why they were about to slap handcuffs on me.

The guy clattered up the steps and snapped a collar not on me but around limp Samantha's neck. Kevin winced as they lifted her onto a stretcher and began to navigate her through the hallway, which was clearly designed by somebody who never planned for a sweet little girl getting carried around its corners on a stretcher.

Kevin followed them down. I grabbed my sneakers, which had been placed emphatically beside my doorway by Joe after I'd left them in the kitchen again. What else? I pocketed my wallet and cell phone. *Think, Charlie. What else? Anything?* I wanted to be responsible. Nothing jumped out at me. As I passed Samantha's room, I considered, for a split second, dashing in to get her shoes or a stuffed animal or a book, maybe look for her bubble gum, but I didn't want to risk getting left behind, so I skipped it.

At the bottom of the stairway, I slid to a stop beside Kevin.

"Who's family?" the EMT guy asked brusquely, his ballpoint pen clicking against the sheet of paper on his metal clipboard.

"I am," Kevin and I both said. The guy paramedic looked down past our faces. So did we—and saw that we were holding hands, fingers interlocked. How did that happen? My sneakers hung from my other hand. Kevin squeezed me one pulse, and I pulsed him back. We didn't let go, just looked at the EMT guy.

"Okay, then," the EMT said, rushing out the front door. "If you say so. None of my business. Let's hustle. You'll need some shoes, son."

I carried my sneakers. Kevin jammed his sock-covered feet into my mother's Ugg slippers and slammed the door shut behind us.

We squeezed into the back of the ambulance, where the woman EMT was doing stuff to Samantha as we lurched away from the curb, sirens blaring. There was an oxygen mask over Samantha's ashen, elfin face.

My phone buzzed. Thinking it was Mom, I checked. It was a text from Tess: *I need to talk to you. In person. Can you come over?*

Sorry, I quickly texted back. *In an ambulance. Something v. wrong with Sam.*

I shut my phone and shoved it back into my pocket. Kevin gripped my empty hand tight as the EMT talked softly to Samantha, explaining that she was checking Sam's blood pressure. Sam did not respond.

Silent tears ran down Kevin's cheeks. *A pretty crier,* I thought; *figures. Not like you and me, Sam.* Still, I held his hand, and held it together, the whole way to the hospital.

thirty-two

A GIRL WHO looked like an exhausted prom-queen/math-nerd hybrid told us in an absurdly British accent that she was the fellow who'd be taking care of Sam.

I considered pointing out that she was clearly not a fellow, so why would she say she was? But she was in her pajamas, poor thing, and also trying to help Samantha, so I didn't say anything. Anyway, I was all smart-mouthed out.

The fellow was gone, then back. Kevin and I were standing like abandoned mannequins in the same place she'd left us. She explained that they were admitting Samantha. This made no grammatical or logical sense to me. I nodded. CT, MRI, MRA, EEG. I nodded more. *Get all the information,* I kept telling myself. Kevin sat down in a chair with his head clutched between his hands, so the fellow and other pajama people were talking to me, until the parents dashed in, frantic—and even after that, I stayed standing, listening, getting all the information. Joe went with Sam; Kevin stayed in the chair; Mom and I took turns pacing and sitting on hard, plastic seats until our butts itched.

Only at three in the morning, when it finally was absolutely confirmed that Samantha was officially not dead, not dying, could I take my first full breath.

I must have dozed off at some point, because the next thing I knew, it was ten a.m. and the fellow who was a woman had come in to escort us to someplace where Joe was already waiting. When we got there, Joe gripped Mom hard and held on as the fellow explained that the attending would be in to see us in a minute. *Please sit down.* So we did. Mom, Joe, Kevin, and I all buzzed in our chairs, yellow jackets whose hive has been kicked.

A doctor in a white coat came into the room and told us her name and her qualifications—attending, neurologist, professor. We didn't care. She could have been the janitor, as long as she gave us some good news.

"She's fine," the doctor said.

"Fine?" Joe asked.

"She's recovering. It seems she had a complicated migraine."

"A migraine?" Kevin asked.

"You know what *migraine* means?" the doctor asked. She sounded exactly like our third-grade teacher asking, *You know what* migrate *means?*

"A really bad headache?" Kevin said in exactly his third-grade voice. I looked at him and he looked at me, and we both started laughing, completely inappropriately.

"Kevin," Joe said. "Please?"

Kevin and I were both convulsed with laughter. "Sorry," Kevin said between gasping laughs. "Inside . . . long story."

Just as abruptly as it had started, the spasm of laughter ended. I hugged my arms around my body; it was so cold in the room my teeth started chattering.

"Her mother gets migraines," Joe said.

"Ah," the doctor said, making a note. "Family history of—"

"She has to lie down in a dark room for two days," Joe interrupted. "Samantha's mother, I mean. I don't think she ever passed out from it."

"Samantha suffered a special kind of migraine, we think," the doctor explained. "Very rare. Basilar-type migraine. Though there's some disagreement over whether that's a misnomer."

"What's the prognosis?" Joe asked. "For Samantha? For basil . . ."

"Basilar-type migraine," the doctor said, clicking her ballpoint pen. "Fine. Excellent."

There was a tremor in Joe's voice as he asked, "So she's okay? She's, it's a *headache*?"

The soft-voiced, sleek-haired doctor nodded, her calm face a universe of patience. Mom paused in taking notes and mumbled, "A migraine." She underlined the word on her black Moleskine pad that had been, as always, in her pocketbook.

"Yes," the neurologist said, and smiled. "Well, basically. Although the symptoms of a basilar-type migraine are very scary to witness, they're not dangerous. No long-term damage or effects. She may have a pretty bad headache for a day or two, and we want to run more tests to be sure that—"

"She's going to be fine, though," Joe interrupted. "The baby is, she's okay."

"Yes," the doctor said. "We want to keep her . . ."

But none of us were listening because Joe was suddenly crying his eyes out, in my mother's arms. And tears were running down Kevin's cheeks, too. I put my hand on his back and rubbed, but then that felt so thoroughly inadequate I gathered him up in a hug.

The doctor waited until we all got ahold of ourselves and then said a bunch more stuff that Mom wrote down in her pad.

I wasn't really paying attention. I was looking at Kevin's feet, which were in my mother's slippers, and his white socks, and loving the fact that he didn't even care because Samantha wasn't dead.

She was napping when we got to her hospital room. Mom said she'd sit with her while Joe and Kevin and I went down to get some food, that a walk-about would do us some good. She asked Joe to bring her a coffee.

In the food line, he picked out a dark chocolate bar with almonds. Mom's favorite. He put it in the bag with her coffee, with a wad of napkins between them as insulation, before we found an open table.

We unwrapped our greasy food and started eating. I was so hungry I didn't even taste anything for a while, but then, with my mouth full, had to admit, "This is the worst grilled cheese I ever ate."

"I make excellent grilled cheeses," Joe said, his mouth full of his turkey club.

"I know," I said. "It's the thing that you're out-of-proportion proud of."

"How did you—" he started to ask.

I cut him off: "Samantha told me. And, you know— family joke," I said. "So, I know. Of course."

And then suddenly I was crying, unprettily, into my disgusting, rubbery grilled cheese, and didn't even care. Because Samantha was going to be fine, and, well, I guess the word *family* got stuck in my throat along with the gloppy grilled cheese. Joe started crying again, too, and then we all three started laughing at ourselves and choking on our gross food.

Joe wiped off his face with a napkin. "And what's your thing, Charlie? That you are out-of-proportion proud of? I should know that."

"Hmmm," I said. "I'm kind of good at tiptoeing."

Kevin hiccupped really loud at that. "No, you're not."

"I think," Joe said, and paused as Kevin hiccupped again, louder. "Maybe your thing is that you stay calm in a crisis."

"Nope. That's pro-hiccup-portional," Kevin objected, which made me and Joe laugh so hard we were crying again.

"What, then? What's my *thing*?"

Then Kevin hiccupped unbelievably louder, and the three of us doubled over laughing, banging our hands on the table, stomping our feet, just so flat-out frigging happy to be alive.

Mom texted Joe that Samantha was waking up. We scrambled to throw out our trash so we could get back upstairs. Sam was going to have to stay over for observation for another night, Joe told us, reading off his phone as we rushed down the hallway toward the elevator, and asked if we were okay taking a cab home together, later, because he and my mom would stay over with Sam. We nodded quietly, remembering for the first time in a long time that there was stuff to sort out there, but pushing that aside for later. It was only noon.

We let the air fill in, between us, a bit.

At the elevator, I realized there was something I had to do. "I'll meet you up there, okay?" I turned to watch the doors slide shut between me and them, then dashed to the gift shop.

thirty-three

WHEN I GOT up to Sam's room, there was a crowd clogging the hallway. A few adults I didn't recognize were chatting with Mom. To the side, surrounding Kevin, was a clump of my friends.

Felicity dashed toward me, helium balloon in hand, and threw her arms around me, hugging me hard and tight.

"Um. Hi," I said, too perplexed to hug her back.

"Oh, Charlie," she breathed. "Are you okay? You totally saved poor Samantha's life!"

"Huh?" I said.

Felicity bent close to me and whispered, "We already heard the whole story from your mom. Don't be humble. You're a hero. Samantha could have died, if it hadn't been for you!"

"Not really," I had to say. "It turns out she just had a migraine."

"If she had died, my goodness," Felicity said, her hand over her heart, tears beginning to sparkle in her eyes as she wrapped her arms around Kevin's neck. He stood there stiffly, looking at me like *What the heck is going on?* while he patted Felicity on her back.

"She didn't die," I said, a little too loud. "She had a headache."

Tess had come toward us by then, with Paige and Darlene, who had nervous smiles on their faces and helium balloons just like Felicity's in their hands.

"How did you even—what are you guys *doing* here?"

"You texted me last night from the ambulance," Tess whispered.

"I did?" I had zero memory of that. I texted Tess? In the middle of everything? What?

She nodded. "So I went by your house this morning to see if everything was okay, because you weren't answering your cell again. Which you know pisses me off. Nobody was around at your house, so I waited for a few hours and then, I just, well, came here."

Kevin had stepped away from Felicity and was standing by my side.

"Why were you calling me?" I asked Tess. "Everything okay?"

Tess nodded. "I guess I just wanted to talk with you. Like always."

"And of course, when we found out where Tess was going,

and why, we all wanted to be here," Felicity said, blinking her big, pretty eyes. "For you, and for Kevin, and of course, for Samantha."

A ball of bile started to well up in my gut, a loud shout of *You are just like every shiny-haired, crying girl in every TV story about a dead teenager—but Samantha didn't die, so leave us alone.*

But that wasn't fair, not really. Maybe she was just trying to be nice. Maybe she just was nice. Also, Kevin had stepped away from her. So what I said was, "Thanks, Felicity."

She hugged me again, then graciously stepped aside to let Darlene and Paige take their turns at hugging me, too. We were like ladies at a luncheon. When Tess hugged me, she held on tight and didn't let go until eventually she straightened up and asked, "When did you get a hammock?"

I laughed. "I know."

"I mean, a hammock?" she asked. "Does anybody ever actually sit in a hammock? On purpose?"

"Some people, I guess," I said, a smile stretching out my unprepared face. "But why?"

"They just droop empty between trees, getting moldy, symbolizing the lifestyle people want to have," Tess said.

This was the conversation I had been wanting to have, with everybody—with Kevin, with my mom. But they didn't go there with me, couldn't, maybe.

"Or think they should want," I said.

"Yes! You're right." Tess beamed. "*Think* they want. But do they really want it? Laziness? That's the goal?"

"Exactly." Tess was a drama queen, it's true, and made me feel bad about myself sometimes in comparison to her—or maybe I couldn't blame her for that, maybe that was on me. Maybe she had even invented the thing about Kevin and Felicity hooking up—they seemed friendly but no more than usual, and Felicity was definitely acting more like *my* friend, there in the hall, than like Kevin's.

But. But Tess could talk about the whys of hammocks and the deeper meanings of types of cookies, and she said she called, all full of crisis—why? Because she wanted to talk to me, *like always*.

"A hammock," I said, "is never just a hammock."

"I know it. *Hammock.* How is that even a word? I think you're supposed to put it in soup."

"I think that's a ham hock," Darlene piped up, which had me and Tess doubled over in laughter.

"Hey," Kevin said behind me. "I like hammocks."

Which totally cracked us up even more. Tess might not be the perfect, flawless, most generous friend, or one I could share all my secrets with, but man, I did love her laugh.

"On the other hand," I said, once I had caught my breath, "I kind of like how it looks, there between those trees. The ham hock. Hammock, I mean."

"You do?" Kevin asked.

I nodded. "It's growing on me."

"Charlie?" my mother called from the doorway of Sam's

room. "Samantha wants to see you."

"Coming!" I managed to not skip up the hall to Sam's room. I yanked open the door, and Samantha grinned as soon as she saw me. She looked little but superstrong in the middle of that white bed. Behind my back I hid the bag that held every last damn piece of bubble gum that the pathetic hospital gift shop had in stock.

As the door closed, Tess yelled to me, "I'll call you later!"

She always used to say, "Call me later." It was a small difference, but nice.

"That would be great," I answered.

thirty-four

"WHAT DID SAMANTHA mean?" Kevin asked me in the kitchen when we were home hours later, staring starving into the refrigerator together.

"About what?" I asked, though I knew what he meant. I didn't want to talk about that, though, so in a rush I went on: "When she said the thing about wanting to be a neurologist if the rock-star chess-champion thing didn't work out? I think she has a little crush on her doctor, or maybe she really—"

"No. Not that."

"No?"

"About forgiveness," he said.

Yeah. That. I studied the back of the orange juice carton. *Lots o' Pulp.* "You really hate pulp?"

"Yes," Kevin said. "Gross. Just before we left. She said you were right about forgiveness."

I closed my eyes and gripped the fridge handle for steadiness. "I told her one time that people forgive each other sometimes."

"Oh."

I pulled out some cucumbers and a hunk of cheddar. "When the parents were fighting a few days ago, and Sam was all stressed."

"And us," he said, taking out the Lactaid milk.

"Maybe." I really didn't want to look at him, so I pulled out the cutting board and started chopping up all the stuff we'd unloaded onto the counter for refrigerator salad.

He pulled out the freezer drawer. "You like pigs in blankets?"

"They make me burp," I said.

"Awesome. Me too," he said. He lined the little hot dogs up in neat rows on the toaster oven tray, his back to me. "Bet I can burp louder."

"No way," I said.

"What do you want to bet?"

Awkward moment. Last bet we'd made had been for a kiss. He'd bet me my mother would love the hammock. I'd won, but not collected a kiss, not even close.

"Bet you that picture," I offered. "The one you drew, of the trees."

"Don't know if you'll want it now."

"Why?"

"I added the hammock."

"Good."

"Yeah? Okay, then, the picture." He clunked the tray into the toaster oven and turned the dial to 350. "What are you putting up, Burp Master?"

"Anything you want."

"Yeah?" he asked softly.

Oh. "Within reason," I hedged.

He smiled without opening his lips, a mercy smile. I knew him well enough now to know where his mind had gone.

"They said it wasn't from stress," I whispered. "That it was just how her brain is. Her brain anatomy or chemistry or something."

"I know."

"It's not our fault."

He turned around. "I know."

I chopped up an onion, which made my eyes water, and then dumped in a half bag of corn from the freezer before starting in on the grape tomatoes.

"You're pretty good with a knife," Kevin said.

"Yeah," I said, chopping a tomato. "So watch out. Hey, maybe that's my thing. Knife skills. That or making tea. I learned how to make a perfect pot of tea."

"Sexy."

"Nobody's asking you, you coffee-drinking heathen. Watch your fingers."

He pulled his hand away, unscathed, but with a stolen

grape tomato dangling like an earring from it. He popped it into his mouth. "I'm starving."

"You can really say all the presidents in order?"

"In under a minute."

"You cannot."

"Time me. Washington/Adams/Jefferson/Madison/Monroe/Adams . . ." On and on, in a rush, all of them.

"Fifty-two seconds," I said. "Very impressive."

"You have an excellent upper back."

"I have what?"

"You do," Kevin said. "Brad noticed last September. It was like the talk of school for a few days. You could be out-of-proportionately proud of that."

"That's a weird—my upper back?" I tried to get a look, over my shoulder. "Is that even a thing?"

"On you it is."

"Huh. Okay. What about my neck? I was thinking maybe I have a nice neck."

"Never noticed," Kevin said. "I don't drink coffee, either."

"I can bend my thumb backward to touch my arm," I bragged, and showed him.

"Ew, that is just disgusting!" Kevin turned his face away. "Never do that again!"

My phone buzzed. I grabbed it, and Kevin crowded in right behind me to read the text over my shoulder, figuring, as I was, that it could be news about Sam. It was Tess, though, asking if everything was okay and if I was still going to see the band tonight with Toby.

I texted back, with Kevin watching:

All good and No.

"You can, if you want," Kevin said.

"I don't want to," I said, finally telling the truth.

"You don't?"

I considered admitting that I was never actually planning to go to a concert with Toby, that Toby had just been a friend in a clutch, a good guy, a good *co-worker*—to buck me up in front of him and my other friends. Because of that whole telling-the-truth idea I kept trying, I took a deep breath and mentally zoomed through all the ways of explaining what I had done.

On the other hand, I decided, I didn't owe anybody a full account of every thought in my head. Not Tess, not my mom, not Kevin.

"I want to eat hot dogs," I said instead.

Kevin smiled. "And burp," he said, checking on the dogs. "Good. Me too. Think I'll call my dad and see how they're doing. Unless, do you want to?"

"You can." I just needed a moment to bask in how well I'd handled that not telling everything but not feeling guilty or betraying about it. I felt weirdly sturdy.

Kevin was shaking his head. "I'm a little phone-o-phobic."

"Yeah," I said, "I noticed that when we had to call nine-one-one."

He stared at me.

"Too soon?"

"Yeah," he said.

"Sorry." I ate half a grape tomato, still sturdy. "Rockin' phobia, though."

He smiled a tiny bit. "Shut up."

"You tell me to shut up a lot."

"Yeah, well," he said. "You deserve it."

"I do not."

"True," he said.

So I threw a grape tomato at his head. It was the most eloquent response I could come up with. Hit him smack in the nose. He threw one back at me. When all the remaining tomatoes were scattered around the kitchen floor, we sank back against the counter.

"My phone is dead," he said.

"Surprise, surprise." I shook my head at him. "I'll call."

Samantha was asleep, as was Joe, so my mother was whispering. The doctors were almost certain Sam would be discharged in the morning.

"You okay there?" Mom asked.

I looked around the ravaged kitchen. "Yup."

"Everything's fine," I told Kevin after I hung up. "Maybe we should go buy Sam a new Betta fish. Or a tortoise? They live for, like, a hundred years. And doesn't she seem like someone who should have a tortoise?"

"Yes," Kevin whispered, his intense blue eyes unblinking. "She does."

The toaster dinged; the hot dogs were done. Neither of us moved toward them.

"I don't know how much they cost," I said. "Tortoises. But I have twenty-one dollars from Cuppa. . . ."

Kevin leaned forward and held out his hand to me.

"What?"

"Come outside with me."

The shiver was starting again deep inside me despite the lingering warmth from the day, as I walked out the back door holding Kevin's hand. Down the hill we went, our bare feet squishing in the cool, damp grass. When had it rained? While we were inside the hospital? I couldn't even remember what day it was.

He stopped at the hammock, dropped my hand, and gripped the side of the swaying thing with both his fists. "Get in."

"No way," I said.

"Way," he answered. "Don't be scared."

"I'm not scared," I said. "I think we have determined for all time who panics and who doesn't in this family."

We froze. It hung there between us. *In this family.*

Damn.

I took a big, greedy gulp of the sweet night air, closed my eyes, and then sat my butt down on the hammock. It swished away from where I'd been, lifting my feet off the ground, swinging me away from Kevin and then back. I may have screamed a tiny bit.

Next thing I knew, I was lying down in the cocoon of it, with Kevin lying beside me. We were rocking from side to side. I closed my eyes to keep from vomiting.

When the rocking settled, I realized Kevin was holding my hand again.

I didn't turn my face toward his, because a truth was blaring in my head, a truth I was not particularly excited about but that I really couldn't ignore anymore.

"Kevin," I whispered. "You know we can't do this."

Instead of shushing me this time, he whispered back, "I know."

"It's not that I don't want to . . ."

"I know," he said. "Me too."

We lay there for a while, not talking, just okay together, his fingers and mine interlaced.

"Kevin . . ." I opened one eye and looked up at the sky with its gaudy array of twinkling stars.

"I didn't hook up with Felicity, by the way."

"That's not what—" I started, though I was, honestly, happy he had confirmed that.

"No, I'm with you, Chuck. We can't be, like, a going-out-in-ninth-grade-for-a-few-weeks-until-we-piss-each-other-off-and-break-up couple."

"Right."

"We're more than that, and different."

"And forever," I added, opening both eyes now.

"Yeah," he said. "That's a concept, huh? Forever?"

We didn't move, except, microscopically, our fingers.

"How are we gonna . . . ?" I whispered.

"Easy," he said, not sounding entirely convinced.

"Yeah?"

He reached his outside arm up and stuck his hand under his head. "We just stay like this, a little bit in love, no more."

"A little bit . . ."

"Or, you know, in a cool space, whatever."

"But just a little. One inch. One ounce. No more."

"Charlie!"

"No, I totally agree."

"You will have to wear big, ugly sweaters all year to hide your back, though."

I laughed. "Only if you don't do that slow-smiling thing."

"What slow-smiling . . ."

"Just, don't smile at me. And definitely don't touch my hair."

"I'll try," he said. "You have this bit that falls over your face sometimes, though, and . . ."

"Off-limits, bucko."

"Okay, and . . ."

I laughed a little. "Yeah? And what else?"

"And, we deal."

I nodded. I didn't feel like crying, or jumping out of my skin, or chattering, or making dumb jokes, or even mashing my face against his. It felt okay to just be there together, hanging out, dealing. More than friends, but not in the less-than-friends way *more-than-friends* had meant before. Really more. "We deal," I agreed.

"We're a good team," he said. "We just—we put some stuff aside, and . . ."

"And keep rowing," I said.

"Yeah. Exactly."

Neither of us said anything for a while. It wasn't even awkward.

"Think we can manage?" he finally asked.

"I know we can." I took a deep breath in. "But I should warn you, in all fairness—every once in a while, you'll probably think of me when you smell the honeysuckle."

"Always," he said.

And then we just lay there together, holding hands and watching the murky universe spin around us for a while.

Acknowledgments

The first fifty to sixty drafts of a book are the hardest for me to write. For their wise guidance and enthusiastic embrace of what this story needed to be through draft after draft, I am deeply indebted to Rachel Abrams as well as Elise Howard and Toni Markiet. Amy Berkower, my extraordinary agent, is not just my business partner but also my friend and pathfinder. I'm so lucky to have her in my corner. My friends sit with me around campfires both real and metaphorical, sharing stories and laughter, for which I am forever grateful. Here in this book that asks *what is a family* and *how do we love one another*, I must acknowledge how blessed I feel to be a part of my "big" extraordinarily loving family of parents, in-laws, siblings, and cousins. To my "little" family, full of inside jokes shared with you three good men who are my home and my heart: I love you beyond measure. Finally, to my readers: Thank you for asking for more from these characters and for embracing them—your passion kept them alive and brought them back. Their journey was charted by me, but powered by you.

kiss me again

A Q&A with Rachel Vail

Take a Character Personality Quiz

A Special Valentine from Rachel

Read an excerpt of *Lucky*,
the first novel in Rachel's Avery sisters trilogy

A Q&A with Rachel Vail

Q: You wrote the first book, *If We Kiss* and *Kiss Me Again* almost eight years apart. What was the hardest part about picking up the story again?

A: The characters never really left me alone—so getting back to them wasn't hard at all. I think probably the most challenging part for me was my awareness of the readers. I normally just focus on the characters, trying to get as compellingly as possible to the truth for them, testing them, pushing them up against the most elemental questions. But I decided to write this sequel because so many readers had written asking me to continue the story—and they had pretty strong ideas about what needed to happen! So for one of the only times in my writing life, I was acutely aware of a very engaged bunch of readers waiting and waiting for something—and I really wanted to make the book both fulfill their hopes and also surprise them at every turn.

Q: Charlie and Kevin have some pretty steamy make-out scenes. What's your secret to writing the perfect kiss?

A: The perfect kiss—now there's an elusive goal. I guess my big secret is just to focus on the details. Take it slow. I ask myself a lot of questions in every moment of the process. What is Charlie thinking, lightning-fast, as Kevin's face moves toward hers? Where did he come from? Their shared bathroom? Are they sharing toothpaste now? Or not? Can she smell the toothpaste on his breath? Those are the tiny bits that make it feel real. As for steamy? Well . . . it's a pretty steamy situation Charlie and Kevin are in. I was never a believer in the "a kiss is just a kiss" idea. Sometimes a kiss can shake your whole idea of the world, and yourself in it.

Q: Tess can sometimes be a great friend, and she can sometimes be a bit hard to love. Have you ever had a friend like Tess? What advice would you give to readers when they find a childhood friendship beginning to change?

A: Of course I have! None of us is perfect; every one of us has hurt and been hurt by a friend, through selfishness, carelessness, or misunderstandings. I think the key is respect—be kind, both to your friends and (this is key, and hard) to yourself. But being kind is not the same as being a doormat. If you discover that you're the one in Tess's shoes (and I've been there)—if you realize you've done something you're not so proud of and ended up hurting a friend—it's hard but good to acknowledge it, apologize, and try to learn from it. When a friend is being consistently hurtful or mean to you, though, and won't own up to it or change how she's acting, it's time to step away. Even if the friend is going through a hard time herself; even if you've been friends for a long time. Sometimes a friendship needs a bit of breathing room to grow and change. But sometimes a friendship that was really important in one time of your life can't be sustained later. There doesn't have to be explosive drama; a quiet step back can feel shattering but also right.

Q: Have you ever made refrigerator salad? If so, what do you normally put in it?

A: All the time! I love refrigerator salad! I think the best additions are cut-up fruit and, in August, corn cut from the

4

cob. I'm not a meat eater or a dressing fan, but refrigerator salad can always be personalized for each member of the family. So everybody has the best version.

Q: Charlie has her fair share of awkward and embarrassing moments: kissing Kevin's forehead, the sex talk with her mom, a miscommunicated fight with Joe. Do you have a most embarrassing moment?

A: Too many to list! The time my top fell off at a dance when I was fifteen was a biggie, awkward kisses mis-aimed and mis-timed, enthusiastic greetings to people who turned out to be strangers instead of friends (must remember to wear my glasses more!) . . . but sadly those aren't the only moments of hideous humiliation I've experienced. I dredge them all up repeatedly for my books, whenever I need to remember the soul-crushing feeling of being embarrassed in front of friends. So at least my experiences are not only horrible—they are useful! No, they are really just constant ego-deflators.

Q: Did you know starting from the first book how Charlie and Kevin's story would end or did the ending change over time?

A: I always know how the book I'm writing will end before I start, but it always changes as I write. (I am always wrong.) I knew, for instance, that there was too much electricity between Charlie and Kevin to keep them completely apart. I knew they would have to explore what this crush they shared on each other would mean, both through the first book and then in the context of being part of a blended family. *What does it mean to be a family?* I kept asking myself while writing *Kiss Me Again*. (Shared inside jokes became a big theme, and routines, plus questions of secrets, loyalty, and multiple kinds of love.) I knew their relationship would be tested, and that it would grow; it would sometimes be steamy, and sometimes just awkward. . . . But where would I leave them? I had a pretty clear idea at the outset but it changed profoundly as I wrote draft after draft after draft.

Charlie and Kevin's story hasn't really ended, though, even now, in my mind—since they will be part of each other's lives forever. It's always funny to me when people ask if they "end up" together. They're only fifteen! They're a long way from endings, although they do find some kind of balance at the end of this book.

Q: How do you really feel about hammocks?

A: I actually really love hammocks. I have been unable to convince Charlie of the obvious fact that hammocks are awesome for naps and reading. Also, cuddling. She and I will have to agree to disagree on this one. Even though obviously she is SO wrong.

Character Personality Quiz

Which *Kiss Me Again* character are you the most like?
Take this quiz and find out if you're like Charlie, Kevin,
Tess, or George!

1. **You're caught in an embarrassing moment. Your response would be**
   (a) Make a joke to ease the tension. Humor always helps!
   (b) Brush it off and play it cool. It's only awkward if you make it awkward.
   (c) Pretend like it was totally on purpose.
   (d) Acknowledge the moment and move on. It can't be that bad, right?

2. **Your all-time fantasy date would include**
   (a) A late night filled with witty banter, great conversation, and kissing.
   (b) A low-key night in, watching old movies or a baseball game.
   (c) A walk on the beach and then dinner under the stars. And fireworks!
   (d) A picnic in the park on a sunny, warm day.

3. **You have a new crush, and you suddenly find yourself flirting like crazy. You show you're into someone by**
   (a) Playing hard to get.
   (b) Subtly touching the other person's hair and whispering.
   (c) Passing him or her a perfectly worded note in class.
   (d) Taking an interest in what he or she likes to do.

4. **It's the first day of school and you're selecting your outfit. You'd wear**
   - (a) Clothes or accessories that let your personality shine through: mismatched socks, colored shoelaces, or a funky piece of jewelry.
   - (b) Your favorite soft T-shirt, jeans, and sneakers—keeping it simple!
   - (c) The season's latest fashions. You're always in vogue.
   - (d) A classic outfit that never goes out of style.

5. **Your perfect kiss would be**
   - (a) Tender, sweet, and private. You only want to share this moment with one person.
   - (b) Spontaneous and passionate.
   - (c) A French kiss.
   - (d) After a great date when you've waited all night long to do some smooching.

6. **You've just gotten into a huge fight with your best friend and you want to make up. What's your next move?**
   - (a) Text her saying that you're "so sorry!"
   - (b) Pretend the fight never happened.
   - (c) Wait till she comes to you. You want to make up, but you're still pretty steamed!
   - (d) Sit down and tell her how you feel.

7. **It's Halloween and all of your friends are going to a costume party. Your perfect costume would be something**
   - (a) Clever: you like to make people think and can turn an everyday item into a unique costume.
   - (b) Classic: you can never go wrong with a scary monster or a witch.

(c) Shared: costumes are the most fun when you team up with a best friend.

(d) Cute and cuddly: everybody loves baby animals!

8. **You're thinking about applying for a part-time job. Where would you want to work?**

(a) At a coffee shop or café.

(b) At an art gallery.

(c) At a stylish boutique.

(d) At the movie theater.

9. **The weekend is finally here! Your go-to plans are**

(a) Hanging out at home and catching up with family.

(b) Going to a friend's party.

(c) Inviting your BFF to your house for a sleepover.

(d) Going on a date.

10. **How do you take your coffee?**

(a) Tea, please!

(b) Black.

(c) Vanilla bean java shake with whipped cream.

(d) Hot chocolate.

Character Personality Results:
Mostly a's: Charlie

Clever and quirky, you're most like Charlie. You always have a witty response to any given situation and you can think on your feet. You sometimes find yourself in some pretty awkward spots, but you trust your instincts to find the right way out. Your creativity, individuality, and strong leadership skills make everyone in awe of you, even if you don't know it!

Mostly b's: Kevin

Artistic and alluring, you're most like Kevin. You have an easygoingness with others that makes you a social magnet, but as a result, you're occasionally at the center of all the drama. However, your thoughtfulness and laid-back sensibilities allow you to stay unruffled and see through the mix to what's most important to you: friends and family.

Mostly c's: Tess

Energetic and confident, you're most like Tess. A passionate friend with a flair for style, you know what you want and how to get it. Your enthusiasm is contagious and brings people together. And even if you do get a little carried away, your strong morals and kindness always find a way to shine through.

Mostly d's: George

Considerate and loyal, you're most like George. Always an optimist, you try to see the best in things and give everyone a fair shot, but you're no pushover. You excel at expressing yourself with honesty and are admired by your friends and family. Your good-naturedness, silliness, and romantic ideals make you a true pleasure to be around.

A Special Valentine from Rachel

Valentines or love letters are not always written to those with whom we are romantic, and they don't need to be written only on Valentine's Day. Because love is bigger than that. Charlie learns that her capacity to love extends much further than to just the boy down the hall. It reaches people who sometimes frustrate her like Tess or Joe or even to Sam, the sister that she never knew she wanted. So, when Rachel Vail was asked to write a valentine, she dedicated it to someone who helped her become the writer she is today, her little brother.

A Valentine for My Little Brother

If I'd tried as a kid to learn how to become a writer, I probably would have worked on my penmanship. And definitely on my spelling. Maybe later I'd have focused consciously, conscientiously, on using sense imagery or similes, and then, in high school, would have aped the styles of my favorite authors. But I didn't want to be a writer. So I didn't bother much with any of that.

Instead I built a time machine in the backyard. There was a mysterious stake stuck in the ground next to a listing tree; what else could it be but the control lever of a top-secret machine that could bring my younger brother and me wherever I said it would? Jon would squeeze in tight beside my left foot and off we'd go. We'd dash around the backyard then, which had transformed into colonial America or medieval England or ancient Egypt. He'd happily follow wherever I said we'd gone. With sticks for swords or muskets or magic wands, we'd fight off bad guys and face down perils until Mom called us in for lunch.

On cold or wet days, we'd have "lessons" in the playroom, where Jon and a bunch of Imaginaries were my students. I taught Jon how to read before kindergarten. Some of the Imaginaries were slower learners than he, and he almost always had more stars beside his name than any of them. Conflicts among the students were discussed (I narrated what was happening, of course) and resolved before snack time. I made the snacks in my Easy-Bake oven, where the "magic potion" (the packet of chemicals that came with the set) was stirred with "super liquid" (water) and baked by the heat of the Easy-Bake lightbulb (it was the seventies) into the most delicious brownies Jon had ever eaten, and not only because they gave him superpowers.

One time we went on a family vacation in the Poconos. There was a Kids Kamp or some such horror, and I quickly, happily, fell in with some slightly older girls I thought were extremely cool. Like, they wore Sassoon jeans level cool. There was a talent show coming up and those girls included me in their group; I was beyond psyched. Together we made up a cheer routine that was pretty much the definition of awesome.

My brother, meanwhile, decided to sing a John Denver song in the show. It was the only thing he was interested in doing for it. He asked a few kids to join him but got only a face-ful of no. Nobody, again, just like at school. No, no, and no. He was the only kid at Kids Kamp without a partner. "That's okay," he said in our room the night before the show, blinking his huge brown eyes. Damn.

So I quit the cheer routine to do "Leaving on a Jet Plane" with Jon instead. We sang it, the parents in the audience clapped, I bowed but Jon wouldn't. "It's not done yet," Jon insisted, loud, into the microphone. People laughed. I died a little. We sang the next verse. Applause, bow, "Come on, Jon; let's go." "It's not done yet." Lather, rinse, repeat. We sang all four billion verses of that stupid song. The cool girls grew up, went to high school and then college, settled down in the suburbs, and had kids of their own all while my brother and I continued to sing about leaving on a jet plane. Without. Ever. Leaving.

And so it went.

But here's the thing: afterward, he wanted me to tell and retell the story of that horror, even though he didn't come out sounding so great in it—and neither did I, obviously. My longing for the cool easy company of those other girls, the uncomplicated exhilaration of friendships that start and end within the week, away, where I could be anyone—I could be someone whose brother wasn't a bit quirky and prone to doing socially weird stuff; I could be someone who'd be in the cool cheer group. But no, there I was, caught onstage with him, in front of everybody, my vulnerability and shame and immature petty embarrassment on display. His stubbornness, his lack of clue about how to go with the flow, how to be cool. The parents whispering to one another, giggling behind their programs. Did that part happen? Or did it only go down that way in the retellings? Did the cool girls actually shun me when I quit their cheer? Did I do the cheer with them and then also do the song with Jon? It's possible, I suppose. But the story became the memory, the grooves of

13

it channeling in my mind so deep that even now, remembering, I can feel again that heaviness in my chest and the ache in my ankles as I willed myself against every instinct to stay there beside my brother instead of fleeing.

Love is complicated. I used to chide myself to be more patient, more generous with my brother. I congratulated myself, privately, for stuff like standing by his side on stages like that one in the Poconos and on other less literal stages as well. But what I may not have realized growing up is how grateful I should have been as well. Just by being the way he was, so adamantly unlike me, so immune to the opinions of others, he taught me about perspective and character: that not everybody saw things the way I did; not everyone will make the same seemingly obvious choice in a given situation; that the kid standing beside me is not playing my perceived scene but is necessarily having a fundamentally unique experience in every moment.

"Tell me again about the time . . ." Jon would say, or "Where are we now?" he'd ask inside the playhouse or hiding beside a rock. And I'd oblige. I'd watch him to see what worked, what twists and details earned his biggest smiles or his widest eyes of anticipation. Through the years, Jon insisted both that I make stuff up and share it with him, and also that I remember, and tell him what happened to us both but better, funnier, truer. Again. More. Four billion verses later I am still standing up here, telling stories.

Because he taught me how.

Read an excerpt from Rachel's book

LUCKY

Book one of the Avery sisters trilogy

IT WAS DARK IN THERE UNTIL I opened the refrigerator door. I grabbed two Sprites and handed them to Luke, but didn't look him in the face. It's not the first time he'd been in the pool house; we have parties all the time and anyway I could see his and William's T-shirts on the bed in one of the rooms, the one to my right. But there we were, in the pool house, dripping wet, alone together.

"You want a towel?" I asked, going quickly around him, trying not to look at his flat stomach and tan chest on my way to turning on all the lights and opening the closet. When did he get arm muscles? I flung a towel back toward him. He caught it on top of his soda cans.

"Phoebe," he said.

I took a breath and forced myself to look up at him. Water was dripping off his hair.

"Yeah?"

He took a deep breath, too, and looked at his feet. "So,

uh, what's going on?"

My mouth opened but nothing came out. Going on? With me and him? Me and Kirstyn? My family? "I honestly have no idea," I whispered.

He smiled, frowned, then smiled again, so quickly that if I hadn't been staring at his face I'd definitely have missed the frown.

"What?" I asked, echo-smiling.

"Nothing, just . . ." He bit his lower lip. "I just know exactly what you mean."

"You do?"

"No." When I squinted at him, he smiled again. "Not exactly, I guess, I mean, but yeah. It's weird, isn't it?"

"What?" I tried to keep smiling, but it was a challenge.

"Everything," he said.

"Yeah," I said. Okay, so here's the thing. He really is incredibly cute. He's fun and hot and maybe Kirstyn was right about me liking him again, and I had just been in denial.

How intense and black are his eyes? Were they always like that?

He isn't the clingy little mama's boy he was when we were five, I thought, but hello, I'm not in a little pink dress anymore, either. And the way I acted to him the first week of seventh grade was so long ago, I was probably remembering it all wrong anyway. Maybe I hadn't been as much of a jerk as I thought. Maybe he'd forgotten, or decided we had all grown up a lot and forgiven me.

There was really nothing stopping us from hooking up, since that's what we clearly both wanted to do.

Well, anything other than the fact that my best friend would think I was crazy, and an idiot, and a loser. But maybe she would never know anyway.

He took a step toward me. We had only kissed a few times, back when we went out in sixth grade, and all those kisses (other than the last one) were in front of everybody, at those dumb parties we used to have. Still, I could remember how soft his lips were, how lightly they brushed mine, so different from gross Dylan Baker at camp with his gross tongue. Ew, I couldn't even think about *him* without gagging; I don't care how tall he was—yuck. So what if Luke is only my height, and wears Old Navy clothes, and maybe doesn't shave at all yet, and his father is friends with my father and we've known each other forever?

Right there in my pool house, on a perfect warm May day, in my best Calvin Klein bathing suit and him in just shorts, smiling at me like that . . . it did not seem babyish and boring to think about kissing him again. The opposite, actually.

"I was wondering," Luke said.

I just waited. I didn't want to mess him up, in case he had it kind of planned out or something.

"Do you have any chips in here?" he asked.

"Chips?"